Cindy couldn't wait to get back on Honor. . . .

"How do you feel?" Ashleigh asked.

"Much better," Cindy lied. "I'm glad you came by. I wanted to talk to you about Honor." To her dismay Jeremy moved closer to Ashleigh and looked very interested.

"I wanted to talk to you about her, too," Ashleigh said.

Honor was hanging her head over the stall door and gently pushing her chest against it. The filly was hoping someone would get the message and take her out.

"She's a beauty." Jeremy stroked Honor's nose. The finicky filly tossed her head and moved away. "But I'll find out what she's really got tomorrow, when I ride her for the first time."

"What?" Cindy gasped. She sank back in her chair, spots bursting before her eyes again.

"We've got to keep Honor on track," Ashleigh said gently. "I needed someone to ride her until you felt better."

Cindy couldn't think of anything to say to Ashleigh. After all, what was there to say? Everything had been decided.

"I really have been replaced," she said softly.

Don't miss these exciting books from HarperPaperbacks!

Collect all the books in the THOROUGHBRED series:

THOROUGHBRED Super Editions:

*coming soon

ATTENTION: ORGANIZATIONS AND CORPORATIONS

THOROUGHBRED

CINDY'S HONOR

CREATED BY
JOANNA CAMPBELL

WRITTEN BY
KAREN BENTLEY

HarperPaperbacks
A Division of HarperCollins*Publishers*

![HarperPaperbacks logo] **HarperPaperbacks**
A Division of HarperCollins*Publishers*
10 East 53rd Street, New York, N.Y. 10022-5299

ISBN 0-06-106493-9

HarperCollins®, ![logo] ®, and HarperPaperbacks™ are trademarks of HarperCollins*Publishers* Inc.

Cover art: © 1997 Daniel Weiss Associates, Inc.

First printing: December 1997

Printed in the United States of America

Visit HarperPaperbacks on the World Wide Web at
http://www.harpercollins.com

❖ 10 9 8 7 6 5 4 3 2

—to John—

THIS CAN'T BE HAPPENING! CINDY MCLEAN SCREAMED silently. With all her strength she pulled back on Honor Bright's reins, trying to slow the galloping Thoroughbred filly. But Honor continued her headlong rush straight for the inside rail of Whitebrook Farm's training track.

"Honor, stop!" Cindy pleaded.

Cindy had been careful during Honor's warm-up, but as she asked her for a gallop the young horse had suddenly bolted. Now Cindy wasn't able to stop her.

The bay filly flung up her exquisite head, whipping streamers of her long black mane into Cindy's face. "Good, you are going to mind," Cindy whispered hopefully. But Honor locked her jaw against the bit and continued galloping.

Cindy could see the grain of the white-painted

wood rail as Honor thundered closer and closer to it. Frantically she hauled on the right rein, trying to turn Honor away from the rail and certain injury.

But the powerful young horse was too much for Cindy's aching arms. Honor was all mindless speed, power, and determination now. The roar of Honor's long-strided, fluid gallop drummed in Cindy's ears as the filly pounded across the track.

She's not going to stop, Cindy realized. *We're going to hit the rail!*

Honor hit the fence at chest level. As the filly burst through to the inner turf course she lost her balance and began to fall. Cindy felt as if she were moving in slow motion as she desperately tried to stay on Honor's back. But she knew her efforts were useless. When Honor went down, she would, too.

The next instant Honor slammed onto her knees. The impact jerked Cindy out of the saddle and forced her over Honor's head. The bright April sunshine sparkled off Honor's gleaming bay coat as the filly tried to rise to her feet, then rolled onto her side with a groan and was still.

An instant later the hard ground rushed up to meet Cindy, and the world dissolved into blackness.

She was running . . . running across a field to Honor, but suddenly the filly was beside her. Cindy wasn't at all surprised. "Come on, girl," she called. "Let's go home!"

The beautiful filly tossed her head and whickered. Looking back, Cindy saw that Wonder's Champion was following them. The dark chestnut colt lunged ahead, throwing a little buck as if to say, "Hurry up!"

Behind Champion, Cindy saw Ashleigh's Wonder. The copper-colored mare whinnied loudly.

Cindy ran faster, trying to keep up with the racehorses. I could go like the wind if I rode any of them, *she thought. She felt a blissful smile stretch across her face.*

Suddenly the lush green acres of Whitebrook came into view. There was Ashleigh and Mike's two-hundred-year-old farmhouse, nestled into tall oaks, and, to the left of it, her family's cozy, white-painted cottage.

Honor, Champion, and Wonder slowed to a trot as they approached the red training, breeding, and stallion barns across the drive from the house and cottage.

We're almost home, *Cindy thought.* I'd better grab Honor's reins so that she doesn't run right into the barn.

Cindy tried to reach up, but for some reason she couldn't move her arm. The next second she screamed with pain. . . .

"Cindy, honey, can you hear me?" someone asked.

Cindy tried to open her eyes. *Dad?* That had sounded like her dad's voice.

"Where am I?" she tried to ask, but her lips would barely move.

"She's coming out of it." Cindy didn't recognize the woman's voice.

"Cindy, can you wake up?" It was her dad's voice again.

Did I oversleep? Cindy thought fuzzily. She tried to move, but a burning, aching pain radiated from her left shoulder all the way to the tips of her fingers. Her ribs hurt terribly every time she breathed. Her eyelids fluttered as she struggled to open her eyes.

"Take it easy, darling. You're in the hospital." It was her mother's voice. Cindy felt a cool hand on her forehead.

Suddenly she remembered the sickening thud of her head on the ground. She vaguely recalled being loaded on a stretcher and the worried faces looking down at her. A long time later she'd woken up in a brightly lit room. A man's voice had said hurriedly, "This doesn't look good. Get her down to X ray."

The bright lights in the room had hurt Cindy's eyes. She'd closed them, grateful to drift off into blackness again.

Now Cindy forced her eyes open a crack. Pain and nausea threatened to drag her down under the surface of light, but she tried to stay conscious. She had to remember—

Honor! Cindy tried to sit up, but the pain in her shoulder and ribs made her sick to her stomach. She sank back onto the pillow, groaning.

A nurse hurried into the room. "Don't pull out

4

your IV," she said, checking the bandage on Cindy's arm.

"Take it easy, sweetheart," Cindy's dad said. "You had quite a fall," he added.

"I know," Cindy whispered. She struggled to make her lips move to ask about Honor, but she was so tired. "What—"

"You gave us a real scare." Beth bent over Cindy's bed.

"Sorry," Cindy muttered. "Tell me . . . "

"You need to stay still," Ian said. "You've got some internal injuries and a few broken bones."

"Honor . . ." Cindy whispered, but no one seemed to hear her weak voice. She felt herself sinking under the waves of blackness again.

"Shhh." Beth sat on the bed beside Cindy and smoothed back her blond bangs. "Just relax. We'll talk later."

For what seemed like a long time Cindy drifted in and out of consciousness. Sometimes she remembered that she had to find out about Honor, and sometimes she just felt like she had to wake up for an important reason.

"Why is she moaning?" Cindy recognized Max Smith's voice. Managing to open her eyes, she saw her handsome, dark-haired boyfriend silhouetted in the doorway of her dark room.

"She's about due for more pain medication," the nurse answered. "I'll go get it."

"Wait . . ." Cindy struggled to clear her head.

"Cindy!" Max hurried to the bed and stood beside it, taking her right hand. "You scared us all. How are you feeling?"

"Not . . . too bad." Cindy tried not to slur her words. The fiery pain in her left arm and ribs seemed to be getting worse with every second. But her head seemed a little clearer. She just had to talk to Max before she lost consciousness again. Cindy looked imploringly into Max's bright green eyes. "Max, I need to know . . ."

"Everything's totally fine," Max said, but he dropped his gaze.

He's not telling me the truth, Cindy realized. Panic welled up in her chest, and her ribs hurt so much, she could hardly breathe. *Are they hiding something from me? Is Honor dead?*

"Cindy, you're awake!" Samantha McLean, Cindy's twenty-year-old red-haired sister, hurried into the room. "Mom and Dad will be right in. We were just outside talking to the doctor."

Tears of fright and worry ran down Cindy's cheeks. "Just tell me what's going on!" she cried.

"She wants to know how Honor is," Ashleigh Griffen said from the doorway. Mike Reese, Ashleigh's husband, was right behind her.

Cindy wasn't surprised that Ashleigh had under-

6

stood what was on her mind. Despite their difference in age, Cindy felt as close to Ashleigh as she did to her own sister.

Cindy stared at the concerned faces surrounding her. "Okay, I'm ready to hear what happened," she said quietly. The nurse approached the bed, holding a glass of water and two pills. "I don't want to take those for a minute," she insisted.

Ashleigh gently squeezed Cindy's right hand. "Don't worry, Cindy—Honor's going to be okay. She's badly shaken up and sore, but nothing's wrong with her that a little time won't cure."

Relief washed over Cindy. A smile curved her lips. "Good—I can't wait to ride Honor in her first race," she murmured.

"Honey, about riding . . . ," Ian said.

"Let her rest," the nurse interjected firmly. "It's what she needs right now."

Cindy swallowed the pills the nurse handed her. Within minutes her pain had lessened, and her remaining aches didn't seem to matter so much.

Honor's okay, she thought drowsily. *Everything's going to be just fine. . . .*

Cindy woke with a jolt. The hospital room was still dark, and it was stifling hot. She licked her parched lips. She needed a drink of water but didn't want to disturb her mother, who was sleeping on a cot next to her bed. Slowly and painfully Cindy inched herself up until she was leaning against the pillows. She eyed the glass of water on the table to the left of her bed. She could almost taste the cool liquid. The IV was still attached to her right arm, but all she needed to do was stretch out her left arm and pick up the cup. . . .

"Cindy, what is it?" Beth asked, instantly beside her. Cindy looked around frantically, trying to determine where the high-pitched screech filling her ears was coming from. It took her a minute before she realized that the horrible sound was coming from her.

Cindy's forehead was covered with sweat, and her throat felt raw. "I . . . I wanted a drink of water," she gasped. Her arm was on fire, and she thought she might throw up.

"Oh, honey," Beth whispered. "Do you want me to get the nurse?"

Cindy managed to nod. Tears streamed from her eyes. She stared at her left arm. It felt limp and heavy. Cindy closed her eyes and focused, willing her arm to move.

Pain radiated through her body as Cindy tried again to lift her arm. But she couldn't even lift it from the mattress. Cindy screamed again, as much from fright as agony. Frantically she reached her right arm across her body and tried to use her good arm to move her left, but that only caused a fresh burst of pain.

The nurse rushed into the room. "Hang on, Cindy." Beth tried to hand her a pill and a glass of water.

"No, you don't understand!" Cindy cried. "My arm—I can't even lift it. . . ."

2

CINDY GROANED, SQUINTING INTO THE BRIGHT SUNSHINE coming through her hospital room window the next morning. She had hoped that she'd feel better today—that the fear and pain of last night could be pushed aside like a bad dream.

But she didn't feel any better, she realized as she stared at her left hand. She tried to curl her fingers and was rewarded by a shot of pain. Cindy felt a sick lump of fear in her stomach.

"Bad, huh?" Samantha asked sympathetically. She was sitting with Cindy while their parents got breakfast in the hospital cafeteria.

"Worse than bad." Cindy winced, very gently rubbing her hurt arm.

"At least you can feel it—that means there's probably no nerve damage," Samantha said reassuringly.

"I can feel it, all right." Cindy winced again.

"Do you want more pain medication?" Samantha asked.

"No, thanks." As much as Cindy was hurting, she didn't want to doze off again. She wanted to get out of the hospital and back to riding as soon as possible. Cindy trusted Ashleigh's word that Honor was okay, but she knew that she and the filly had a lot of work to do after this disaster. Honor was almost certain to be frightened and upset after her bad experience on the track. Cindy would have to make sure the filly had her confidence back, and Honor's first race wasn't that far off.

"I'll feel a lot better once I can ride," she told Samantha. "I can't afford to miss too much time with Honor."

"Cindy, you're not going to be riding Honor right away," her dad said. Cindy looked up and saw her parents and a doctor she hadn't met before standing in the doorway. Ian and Beth looked worried and sad, and the doctor was shaking his head. Cindy's heart began to pound.

"What . . . what do you mean?" she stammered. "I know I can't start riding this week, but Honor's first race isn't until the end of the summer. I have a little time, don't I?"

Ian sat down on the bed. "Sweetheart, listen to me. You took a tough fall. Your spleen is bruised, you cracked some ribs, and . . . and you hurt your arm very badly."

11

"But it's going to get better, right?" Cindy stared at her dad in shock.

Ian turned to the doctor. "This is Dr. Martin, an orthopedist. He specializes in treating broken bones, and he can tell you better than I can what's going on."

The doctor, a young man with prematurely gray hair, gazed at Cindy with a stern expression. "You've fractured the humeral head in your arm—in other words, broken your shoulder," he said. "The good news is that it's a simple break—a straight line. You didn't shatter the bone. That's amazing after the hard fall you took. You must have strong bones." He smiled encouragingly.

Cindy tried to smile back, but her mouth was trembling too much.

"The bad news is that it's too early to predict how much your arm will recover," the doctor said. "You're young, so your chances of a complete recovery are good. But how well you do will depend a lot on you."

"I'll do anything to get better." Cindy's voice shook. "Just tell me what to do."

The doctor spoke slowly, as if he wanted to make sure each word sank in. "We'll start you on physical therapy as soon as possible. But for the next four to six weeks you'll have to wear a sling, and your arm movement will be very limited."

"That's a month or more!" Tears of pain and fright blurred Cindy's eyes. "What about riding? I have to go back to it soon so that I can ride Honor in her maiden race."

Her father shook his head. "Cindy, that's out of the question. You won't be riding until next fall, at the very earliest."

"No!" Cindy tried not to cry. "That can't be right! You heard the doctor—I have strong bones. I'll heal quickly."

"Cindy, you're going to have to be patient." Beth's voice was very gentle but firm.

"If you stress your shoulder, it could shatter, and you'll end up with a very serious break requiring surgery," Dr. Martin said. "And your spleen must heal or you'll start bleeding internally. I'm sorry, but riding is out of the question for now."

"I know it is right now, but—I mean—in a week or two—I . . ." Cindy let out her breath in a gasp. The doctor's words just wouldn't sink in.

"Cindy, he's not saying you can't ever ride," her dad said quickly. "You've got to think positively."

"That will help your recovery," Beth added.

Cindy barely heard her parents. Exhausted from the news and her own protests, she lay back and closed her eyes. "Give her some time," she heard her mother whisper.

"We'll be right outside if you need us, honey." She heard her father's footsteps as he moved to the door. But she couldn't even bring herself to say good-bye. She just wanted to shut everyone out.

13

*   *   *

"There's the patient," Heather Gilbert announced that afternoon as she walked into Cindy's hospital room. Heather wore a green sundress with matching sandals and a floppy white hat. Her ash blond hair was pulled back in a low ponytail.

Cindy smiled wryly at her best friend. "You look nice—like you should be at Ascot or something."

"Thanks!" Heather smiled back. "This is the latest from Racing Silks." Heather had recently gotten a part-time job at the popular clothing store at the mall.

Max popped his head in the doorway. "Hey, Cindy," he said.

"Hi." Cindy pushed her hair out of her face and looked away, embarrassed. Heather's great outfit only made Cindy more aware of her own looks—she hadn't had a shower since they'd brought her into the hospital three days ago, and her hair was totally tangled. Instead of a pretty sundress, she was wearing a shapeless white hospital gown.

"Anyone for pizza?" Max asked. He set a large flat box on Cindy's night table.

"You bet!" Cindy sat up eagerly in bed. She realized she was starving.

Max kissed her forehead as he sat down next to her. He passed around plates, napkins, and slices.

Cindy bit into her slice, savoring the salty taste of

14

pepperoni and olives. "Mmmm, this is great," she said, swallowing and taking another big bite.

"I thought a pizza might make you feel better," Max said. "Last night when I came to visit you, I took a look at your dinner tray. It was enough to make anybody sick."

"So how are you doing today, Cindy?" Heather asked.

Cindy put her slice down on her plate. "Not too bad."

Since this morning, when the doctor had given her the news about riding, Cindy had done a lot of thinking. If she could just get home, she was positive she could get better faster—a lot faster than the doctor thought. At the very least she could be around Honor. As long as they were together, things would be fine when they started back on their training program.

"Are you mad at Honor?" Heather asked.

Cindy shook her head. "Mad at Honor? No, not at all. I just hope she's not mad at *me*—I let her get away, and she had an awful experience."

"So you think it won't happen again?" Max asked.

Cindy shrugged her good shoulder. "I think I need to be a little firmer with her. But jockeys fall—they all do. I just have to accept that."

"At least you hurt your left arm," Max said. "Since you're right-handed, that won't be as bad."

"Yeah, that's true." Cindy was sure she could

manage. "I'll be fine once they let me get up and move around."

"I guess you're going crazy just lying there." Heather looked at Cindy appraisingly.

Cindy blushed. "I'm dying for a shower," she confessed. "I bet I look totally gross."

"No, you don't," Max said quickly. "A little tired, that's all."

"Oh, yeah, tired," Cindy scoffed. But she smiled at her boyfriend. No matter what, Max was always her biggest supporter.

"Maybe this will help." Heather reached into her large tote and pulled out a plastic bag. "I bought you a new fashion statement for your wardrobe."

Cindy struggled to open the drawstring bag with one hand. Max reached over and helped her. "Oh, a Churchill Downs T-shirt!" Cindy said with delight. "That's great, Heather! My old one is worn out—you can't even read the letters anymore."

"It's super big so you can get your arm in without moving it much." Heather unfolded the dark green T-shirt.

"Thanks, Heather—that ought to work." Cindy smiled broadly. She felt excited and hopeful. "I'll be sure to wear this shirt once I'm riding again," she said.

Heather and Max looked at each other. "Cindy, you'd better take it easy," Max said.

"I can't—I have to ride this summer," Cindy said

firmly. "And that's that. So what's been going on at school?"

Heather laughed. "The usual," she said. "Ms. Stoddard says I have a bad attitude about math."

"You do." Cindy grinned, forgetting her worries for a moment.

"Everybody's asking about you, Cindy," Max said. "When do you think you'll get out of the hospital?"

"I don't know. Soon, I hope." Cindy hoisted herself up in the bed with determination.

"Hey, why don't you try on the T-shirt?" Heather asked. "Then you won't look like a patient when the doctor sees you."

"Sounds good." She was dying to get out of the baggy hospital gown.

"Leave us for a minute, Max," Heather instructed.

"Just call me when you're ready," Max said, leaving the room.

"We will." Heather handed Cindy the shirt. "Here you go."

Cindy examined the shirt, wondering where to start in putting it on. Slipping off the sling and using her right arm for support, she eased her left arm into the sleeve.

"Now put your head in," Heather said.

Cindy tried to pop her head through the neck hole. But no matter how far she ducked her head, she couldn't reach it—not without raising her left arm at least a little. The slash of pain in her arm warned her to stop, but she ignored it. It shouldn't hurt to raise her arm just a tiny bit.

Heather reached over and tried to tug the shirt over Cindy's head.

"Don't," Cindy gasped. Sweat was running down her face. Her shoulder hurt so much, she felt like someone had lit a fire inside it. Cindy collapsed back on the bed.

"I guess I should have gotten you a button-down shirt," Heather tried to joke, but her expression showed how worried she was.

Cindy tried to smile, but she felt like bursting into tears. She couldn't even dress herself—what would happen once she got home?

"Are you okay?" Heather asked.

Cindy nodded. "I just need to rest for a minute," she said.

Max stuck his head back into the room. Cindy could see that he knew what had happened. "Don't worry about it," he said softly, crossing to the bed. "It's no big deal."

"That's right," Heather agreed. Awkwardly she put the T-shirt back in her tote. "I'll save this for when you get home."

"Okay. Thanks, Heather." Cindy really did appreciate her friend's effort to cheer her up.

"I've got to get to work," Heather said. "But I'll come back tomorrow."

Max touched his lips to Cindy's in a gentle kiss. He drew back. "I'll see you tomorrow, too."

"That'll be nice." She reached up with her good arm and hugged Max. Even though she knew she should rest, Cindy didn't want her friends to leave. She knew she would just lie in her bed and worry.

Waving to Max and Heather as they walked out the door, Cindy drew a deep breath. "Relax, relax," she murmured. She knew that tension and fear would only magnify the dull ache in her arm. She lay in the bed and tried to picture what was going on at Whitebrook. Slowly the pain was receding—as long as she held her arm absolutely still.

A breeze ruffled the blinds on the small, rectangular window. Cindy gazed longingly at the patch of clear blue sky and the warm yellow sunshine touching the foot of her bed. For just a moment she imagined she could smell the the clean scent of sun-warmed horses as they grazed in the pastures at Whitebrook.

"What are you doing right now, Honor?" Cindy whispered. "Are you okay?"

Cindy closed her eyes. A burning desire to be back on Honor filled Cindy, as strong as her pain had been a moment before. She stared at the window as if she could fly through it. Honor was headstrong and excitable, but Cindy was sure she could get through to her. *We both just need another chance.*

3

A FEW DAYS LATER CINDY SAT IN THE FRONT SEAT OF HER dad's car, eagerly looking out the window. She had been released from the hospital that morning, and they were only a few miles from Whitebrook now. She gritted her teeth when they hit a bump, jolting her arm in the sling. "Can you go a little slower?" she asked her dad.

Ian glanced over at her. "Sure, honey."

Cindy clutched her arm, trying to hold it steady. But she knew she couldn't complain, or her dad might turn the car around and take her right back to the hospital. Cindy's doctor hadn't been happy about releasing her this soon. He'd issued a lot of warnings. She wasn't supposed to move her arm at all so that the break could heal. Cindy had nodded rapidly after everything the doctor said, hoping she seemed

20

sincere. She just wanted to get out of the hospital and start her own rehabilitation. She figured that once she was on her own, she'd be moving her arm within two weeks, tops.

"I can't believe I'm finally home," she said to her dad.

Ian patted her knee. "I know it's been hard for you. But remember—you still have to be extra careful."

"I know, I know." Cindy smiled excitedly as she saw the first fields of Oakridge Meadows, a farm near Whitebrook.

"I'll talk to Ashleigh about Honor the minute we get home," she said. "I've got some ideas about her training so she won't get away from me again."

Ian frowned. "Cindy, you're not going to be riding for a long time. Didn't you hear what the doctor said?"

"Sure," Cindy said quickly.

The car rolled over a rise and Whitebrook burst into view. Cindy smiled broadly as she saw the bright green paddocks, filled with mares and young foals, and the familiar red barns. "There's Glory!" she cried.

The big gray stallion's ears pricked, and he whinnied after the car. "He knows I'm home," Cindy said delightedly.

Ian laughed. "It seems that way."

Champion was in the paddock next to Glory, the sun picking out highlights in his dark brown coat. A Triple Crown champion, the colt hadn't raced since his stunning success in the Dubai World Cup. Cindy watched Champion restlessly stamping up and down the fence line. "I know how you feel, fella," she muttered.

"Just let me out of this car," she exclaimed happily as her dad parked. Cindy hadn't walked in days. Even when she was leaving the hospital, the staff had insisted on rolling her out to the car in a wheelchair.

"Where's Honor?" she asked, flinging open the car door.

"In the barn," Ian replied. "We put her up because we thought you'd want to see her."

"I could have gone out to the paddock." Cindy swung her legs out of the car and tried to stand. To her amazement, her legs crumpled under her. She grabbed onto the car seat with her good arm, trying to steady herself, but her legs just wouldn't hold her weight. Cindy sank down slowly to the ground. The movement of getting out of the car had jolted her left arm again, and the pain was so bad, she saw spots before her eyes.

"Cindy!" Her dad's arms were around her. "Just relax, sweetheart. I'll carry you to the house."

"No, I want to go to the barn." Her head was slowly clearing and the pain was pushed aside by a wave of fear. How could she take care of Honor if she couldn't even get out of a car?

"You need to rest," her dad argued. "Come on, Cindy. You just got out of the hospital. You can see the horses tomorrow or later this afternoon, after you have a nap."

Cindy saw Max hurrying over to the car from the barn. She had called him from the hospital to tell him she'd be coming home, and he'd promised to meet her here. Cindy realized he must have seen what just happened. "I can take her down to the barn," he said to Ian.

"Dad, please let me go!" Cindy heard a hysterical edge to her voice, but she couldn't help it. She just had to see Honor.

Ian sighed. He looked at Max. "Okay, you can take her down there, but try to keep her quiet."

"I will," Max promised.

"I'll be fine, Dad." Cindy let out a soft sigh of relief as Max carefully picked her up.

"At your service," he joked.

Cindy snuggled in his arms, dropping her head into the crook of his neck. "This isn't so bad," she said.

"Hey, I'll be your workhorse any day." Max squeezed her gently. Walking slowly, he carried her into the training barn.

The barn was cool and dim after the warm sunlight outside. Cindy lifted her head and squinted, trying to see Honor. The filly was nowhere in sight. "Honor?" she called urgently. "Where are you? Are you lying down?"

With a throaty whicker the beautiful filly popped

her head over the stall door. Her dark eyes were anxious and hopeful, as if she'd given up on ever seeing Cindy again.

Cindy felt her insides melt with relief just at the sight of the filly. "Oh, girl, I've missed you so much," she cried.

"Where should I put you?" Max asked. "There's really nowhere to sit."

Cindy slid out of his arms. "It's okay. I can walk," she said. Her knees threatened to give out again, but this time she was ready and caught herself. Walking stiff-legged, she tottered to Honor's stall.

"I'll get you a chair," Max said. "Then you can sit right in front of the stall."

Cindy almost fell onto Honor's stall half door. She grabbed the top to steady herself. "Hi, sweetheart," she whispered.

Honor stepped closer. The filly gently touched her soft black muzzle to Cindy's cheek.

"Everything's going to be okay now," Cindy murmured. She longed to brush the filly's black forelock off the perfect star on her forehead. She knew she'd fall if she let go of the stall door with her right hand, though.

With a small snort Honor pushed against the stall door, as if to say, "Aren't we going out now that you're here?"

"I can't take you anywhere right now, girl." Cindy's legs began to shake from the effort of standing, and she felt herself slowly slipping to the floor. She clutched the stall door, digging her fingernails into the wood, but she was still losing her grip. "In fact, I think I need to rest for a little while."

"Here." Max set up a folding chair in front of Honor's stall and quickly helped Cindy into it.

"Thanks, Max." She bowed her head, willing the waves of nausea and pain to subside.

"There's my pretty filly," Cindy heard a strange male voice say.

Startled, she jerked up her head. A dark-haired man who didn't look much older than Max stood at Honor's stall, patting her nose. Honor had shied away a little from the stranger, but not as much as Cindy would have expected.

"Who are you?" she asked bluntly.

"Jeremy Correl." The man stepped over to her chair and put out his hand. "Nice to meet you. I already know who you are, of course."

Cindy shook hands with Jeremy and so did Max. Max looked at Cindy quizzically, but she just shrugged. Although Jeremy looked vaguely familiar, Cindy didn't know who he was, or what he was doing there.

"Cindy! You're home!" Ashleigh hurried down the stable aisle, a cheerful smile on her face. Christina, her three-year-old daughter, skipped beside her. "Welcome back," Ashleigh said.

"Welcome back," Christina repeated. She had blond

hair like her dad, but her hazel eyes and expressions were very much like Ashleigh's. Christina sat down on the stable floor and began to arrange bits of straw into a tepee.

"Thanks, guys," Cindy said.

"How do you feel?" Ashleigh asked.

"Much better," she lied. "I'm glad you came by. I wanted to talk to you about Honor." To Cindy's dismay Jeremy moved closer to Ashleigh and looked very interested.

"I wanted to talk to you about her, too," Ashleigh said. "Did you meet Jeremy?"

Cindy nodded, glancing at Jeremy. Suddenly she knew where she'd seen him before. "Aren't you a jockey?" she asked.

"Yep," Jeremy replied. "I've been riding for Townsend Acres on the West Coast. I'm Lavinia's cousin."

Cindy gazed at him warily. She had never liked the owners of Townsend Acres, a huge Thoroughbred breeding and training farm. But the Townsends owned half of Wonder and all her offspring and great-offspring, including Honor.

"So are you here to check up on Honor?" Cindy asked Jeremy as politely as she could. She knew she had to accept that Honor was one of the Townsends' horses.

"Yes, as a matter of fact I am," Jeremy replied.

"She's something, isn't she?" Cindy couldn't keep

herself from asking. She wouldn't mind hearing praise for her favorite filly—even from a Townsend.

Honor was hanging her head over the stall door and gently pushing her chest against it. The filly was hoping someone would get the message and take her out.

"She's a beauty." Jeremy stroked Honor's nose. The finicky filly tossed her head and moved away. "But I'll find out what she's really got tomorrow, when I ride her for the first time."

"What?" Cindy gasped. She sank back in her chair, spots bursting before her eyes again.

"We've got to keep Honor on track," Ashleigh said gently. "I needed someone to ride her until you felt better."

Cindy shook her head. Why would Ashleigh have gone to the Townsends to find a rider?

"What about you?" Cindy asked. "Why can't you ride Honor?"

Ashleigh smiled. "I've got a good reason. I'm pregnant again! Christina's going to have a little brother or sister."

"That's . . . just wonderful," Cindy stammered. "Wow, congratulations, Ashleigh. But . . ."

"Jeremy's got a lot of experience," Ashleigh continued. "He's ridden mostly on the West Coast, at Hollywood Park, Santa Anita, and a few other tracks. He won a grade-one stakes at Hollywood Park just last month."

Cindy could feel Max's sympathetic gaze on her, but she couldn't think of anything to say to Ashleigh. After all, what was there to say? Everything had been decided.

"Cindy, you'll have plenty of time to ride next fall, when your arm heals up," Ashleigh said. "This isn't the end. We'll see how it goes for you and put you back on a horse the minute you're fit enough. In the meantime I'm glad Jeremy can help us out; he's an excellent jockey."

Cindy tried to smile. "Sure," she said. "That's good."

Jeremy touched Cindy's right shoulder. "Hang in there," he said.

"Sure," she repeated automatically. Her head was starting to pound, and her vision was getting blurry. She prayed she wouldn't be sick or pass out in front of everybody.

"I'll catch you a little later, Cindy," Ashleigh said.

Ashleigh and Jeremy headed back to the stable office, talking. Christina glanced up, then followed her mother. "Don't worry about Honor, Cindy," Jeremy called back. "I'll come back down and put her out in the paddock."

"Um, okay," Cindy replied. "I really have been replaced," she said softly.

"Jeez." Max shook his head. "I'm sorry, Cindy."

"Me too." Cindy couldn't believe Ashleigh would hire another rider without talking to her first.

Honor leaned over her stall door. The pretty filly bobbed her head encouragingly.

"I know, you want me to pat you." A tear dropped on Cindy's jeans. "I can't, girl." After the shock of the bad news, she felt even weaker than she had before. There was no way she could get out of her chair right now to go to Honor.

Sadly Cindy stretched out her good arm, reaching for the filly, but she wasn't close enough to touch her.

"Want me to carry you over there?" Max asked.

"No." Cindy knew that somehow, by a sheer act of will, she had to stop letting people carry her. As long as she acted like an invalid, people would keep treating her like one.

"So what do you think about this deal with Honor and Jeremy?" Max asked.

"I think it's going to be awful for her and for me," Cindy replied. "Honor doesn't even like him."

"She doesn't really know him, does she?" Max asked hesitantly. "Maybe she'll get along with him better after he's ridden her."

"Maybe." Cindy closed her eyes. She felt terrible. Tomorrow she wouldn't be able to do anything but watch as a stranger rode Honor.

"Cindy? It's me," Heather said that evening over the phone.

"Hi." Cindy tried to stifle a huge yawn. The ringing of the phone had woken her from a sound sleep.

"You sound like you just woke up," Heather said. "Is it hard to sleep with your arm like that?"

"Kind of." Cindy sat up and swung her legs over the side of her bed, wondering if she could walk. "But it's great to be home. I'm sleeping a lot better here."

"Yeah, you should get well fast now," Heather agreed. "So, are you going to school tomorrow?"

"Um, not tomorrow—maybe by the end of the week." Cindy knew she wasn't strong enough to make it through a school day.

"Remember how I promised to throw a party to celebrate your winning the Dubai World Cup?" Heather asked. "But we never got around to doing it."

"The last couple of weeks have been busy, to say the least," Cindy said wryly.

"Well, now's the perfect time to have a party—if you're up to it," Heather said. "We can celebrate your win in Dubai and have a welcome home party, too."

Cindy felt a lump form in her throat. Her friend always knew when she needed cheering up.

"We could have the party next weekend, at Whitebrook," Heather continued. "I already talked to your mom, and she said it was okay with her if you thought you felt up to being the guest of honor."

"That sounds great, Heather." Cindy hoped she

sounded enthusiastic enough. Maybe a party *would* lift her spirits.

"That's settled, then," Heather said. "Now what's your next big step in rehab?"

Cindy groaned. "I don't know. The doctor doesn't even want me to start using my arm for a month."

"You'll go crazy just sitting around for the next month," Heather exclaimed.

"Who said anything about sitting around?" Cindy said. "I've got to be out at the track tomorrow. Ashleigh's trying out a new rider on Honor."

"That's going to be hard for you to watch, isn't it?" Heather asked.

"It's even worse. The new jock is Lavinia's cousin, Jeremy."

"What?" Heather sounded shocked. "Has Ashleigh lost her mind?"

"I couldn't believe it, either," Cindy said.

"Still, Ashleigh wouldn't knowingly put a bad rider on Honor," Heather pointed out. "At least see how it goes with Jeremy. Then you can make up your mind."

"I guess that's all I can do." Cindy bit her cuticle hard. "I just have to believe Ashleigh knows what she's doing. One more bad ride could end Honor's racing career before it even starts."

4

THE SHRILL SOUND OF HER ALARM CLOCK STARTLED CINDY out of a deep sleep. Without thinking she rolled over to her right side and tried to bring her left hand up to hit the off button. The sudden pain in her shoulder jolted her upright, gasping and blinking back tears. The alarm's insistent beep finally cut through the fog of pain, and Cindy carefully reached out with her right hand and silenced the clock.

She leaned back against her pillows, trying to ignore the stabbing pains in her shoulder and arm. "Deal with it," she ordered herself.

At 4:30 A.M., her room was still dark. Cindy had set the alarm to go off extra early so she wouldn't miss a minute of Jeremy's first ride on Honor. She slowly got out of bed and walked to her dresser. Even opening the drawer with one hand was hard—she had to pull on one side with her right hand, then move to the other side and pull.

Cindy took a freshly laundered button-down from the drawer and frowned. "I look like such a dork in these shirts," she muttered, wistfully eyeing the neatly folded T-shirts in the drawer. Keeping her left arm stiff at her side, she pulled the shirtsleeve up over it.

Now for the hard part. Keeping her left arm as motionless as possible, she brought the sleeve halfway up it, then tried to quickly stick her right arm in the other sleeve. The shirt dropped to the floor.

Cindy groaned with frustration. "I can't do anything!" she cried. Her mouth set in determination, she picked up the shirt for another try.

"Need some help?" Samantha appeared in the doorway.

"Yes," Cindy said gratefully.

Samantha came into the room and quickly helped Cindy into her shirt, then buttoned it for her.

"Thanks, Sammy," Cindy said when she was finally dressed and had on her sling. "I feel like the day's half over already."

"Well, lucky for you, it's only just begun!" Samantha gave her a quick smile. "Let's go downstairs and grab something to eat, then get out to the barn."

Cindy sat at the table and looked out the window as Samantha got breakfast ready. The sun was just rising, bathing the barns and paddocks in hazy, golden light. Len, the farm manager, was leading the mares and foals out to the paddock. Two tiny foals, a black and a chestnut, trotted at their mothers' sides, trying to keep up with the mares. Cindy grinned. She loved spring at Whitebrook.

"So what's on your list for today, Sammy?" she asked, taking a bite of cereal.

"I'll probably ride Fleet Street and some of the other two-year-olds," Samantha said.

"You could exercise Honor," Cindy suggested.

"I could, but I'm not a jockey." Samantha shrugged. "Someone else would have to ride her eventually."

"I better get going if I'm going to watch the workout," Cindy said, getting up from the table. "Catch you later, Sammy."

Samantha nodded. "I'll be down in a minute."

Cindy rushed out the door. By now she knew better than to try to run—the jostling motion would kill her—but she walked as fast as she could.

Cindy's breath came shorter and faster as she walked, and finally just before she reached the track, she had to slow down. The familiar black spots swam before her eyes, and Cindy knew she was in danger of blacking out. "Not now!" she said angrily.

Sitting on the ground, Cindy dropped her head between her knees and took deep, slow breaths.

"Are you all right?" Vic Teleski, one of Whitebrook's

grooms and exercise riders, stood over her. He was leading Freedom's Ring, a four-year-old colt. Freedom bent his black head to sniff Cindy's hair, as if he wondered if she were all right, too.

"I'm just fine!" she said faintly.

Vic hesitated. "Okay," he said. "If you say so."

Cindy listened to Freedom's hooves clop on the hard-packed ground as the pair moved away. *Get up!* she ordered herself. If she didn't get down to the track, she'd miss Honor's workout completely. "On the count of three," she whispered. "One, two . . . three!"

Cindy lurched to her feet, staggering crazily.

A strong hand gripped her arm. "Let me help you," her dad said.

"No! I can make it," she protested, secretly glad for the steadying hand.

"Cindy, don't be foolish." Ian's voice was low but firm. "If you fall, you could set back your recovery for weeks. Either you let me help you to the track, or I'm taking you back to the house."

"All right," Cindy said reluctantly.

"Take small, slow steps," her dad said, his arm firmly around her waist.

Cindy's face burned with humiliation as she and her dad approached the gap. Almost all the Whitebrook exercise riders and trainers were there. Vic, Mark Collier, and Philip Marshall had all mounted up and were receiving instructions from Ashleigh and Mike. Jeremy stood a little ways off, checking over Honor's tack.

"Here you go, sweetheart," Ian said. He stopped next to the fence.

Cindy grabbed hold of the top board, trying to catch her breath. Her heart hammered against her sore ribs. She quickly looked over at Jeremy, but he hadn't even seemed to notice her. With a quick motion he swung into Honor's saddle and let her walk off.

Cindy felt a wave of jealousy. It was supposed to be *her* up there!

"Hey, Cindy." Ashleigh walked up behind her. "How are you doing?"

"Okay, I guess." Cindy managed to smile. She wasn't mad at Ashleigh anymore. Given the circumstances, she knew Ashleigh hadn't had much choice about Jeremy. "How are *you* feeling?"

Ashleigh smiled. "Fine, thanks."

"When is the baby due?" Cindy wondered how Ashleigh could bear to give up riding for a year.

"Not until next January."

"That'll be really nice, Ashleigh," Cindy said sincerely.

"Well, I am sorry I'm not riding Honor." Ashleigh frowned. "Given everything that's happened, this does seem like kind of bad timing."

"I'm sorry I let you down," Cindy said miserably.

"Don't be so hard on yourself," Ashleigh said.

Cindy nodded. She could tell Ashleigh honestly felt bad about what had happened.

"I really think the arrangement with Jeremy is going to work out," Ashleigh went on. "So I've entered Honor in the Debutante at Churchill Downs at the end of June."

"That's less than two months away." Cindy stared at Ashleigh in surprise. "I thought you planned to point Honor toward races at Saratoga in August."

"Honor's ready to race now," Jeremy said.

Cindy swung around. Honor and Jeremy stood just a few feet away. "Oh, really?" Cindy said fiercely. "And what makes you the expert?"

"Just watch how well she works today," Jeremy said confidently.

"We'll watch together, Cindy," Ashleigh said reassuringly.

Cindy studied Honor critically. The filly seemed a little confused by the bustle on the track and the strange rider on her back.

Jeremy pulled on Honor's left rein. The filly turned and moved out across the track at a quick walk.

"I'm with you in spirit, girl," Cindy murmured. Ashleigh patted her arm.

"What's she doing today?" Cindy asked.

"Mostly just warm-ups. She hasn't been out since you got hurt," Ashleigh replied. "But I did tell Jeremy he could breeze her a quarter mile if he thinks she's going okay."

The lovely filly burst into a trot and rounded the first turn. Cindy stared longingly after her.

Although the morning was warm, Cindy shivered and drew her jacket tighter across her chest. It had been almost a week since her injury—she had expected to be feeling better by now.

Cindy tried to push away a creeping sense of doubt. The doctor had said she'd probably get back a full range of movement with her arm. But he didn't know how much strength she needed in her arm, and how precisely she had to move it, to ride racehorses.

"Here comes Honor!" Ashleigh said cheerfully.

Cindy stared hard at the track. Honor was rounding the far turn at a gallop, sweeping by Vic on Freedom as if they were motionless. With every stride Honor dug her hooves into the soft dirt of the track, then soared unbelievably high, almost flying.

Jeremy leaned forward at the quarter pole, asking Honor for more speed. In an instant Honor roared into a full racing gallop. Cindy hadn't thought Honor could increase the length and power of her strides, but suddenly the filly was blazing across the track, whipping by the marker poles.

Cindy knew how that would feel. For an instant she could almost believe she was with Honor, leaning over the filly's gleaming bay neck.

Jeremy raised his whip. "She's already running full out," Cindy cried. "Why is he hitting her?"

"He's just straightening her out." Ashleigh was watching closely, too. "He won't hurt her, Cindy. But she's got to learn to keep a safe distance from the rail."

Honor swept by the gap. Cindy noted with alarm that the filly was soaked with sweat, and her breath came in raw gasps. "Didn't he take too much out of her?" Cindy asked urgently. "She hasn't been worked in a week."

"Maybe a little. I told him to use his judgment," Ashleigh said. "Let's see how she comes out of it."

Cindy was already moving toward the gap, gripping the fence to help herself along. Jeremy rode up to the gap and dismounted in a quick, fluid motion.

"Hi, baby!" Cindy rushed to Honor's head, her concern for the filly overshadowing the effort of crossing the track.

The filly dropped her head, blowing hard. Cindy tried to touch her muzzle, but Honor yanked it away and skittered sideways. "Easy, girl," Cindy soothed. "You're okay."

Honor bounced on her hind legs, half rearing. With a loud snort she followed Jeremy over to Ashleigh.

Cindy gazed after them. "Jeremy could have gone a little easier on her," she murmured. "He should have known she'd need a little extra TLC today."

She walked slowly over to where Ashleigh stood with Jeremy and Honor. Now that the excitement was over, Cindy's legs felt weak and shaky. She was embarrassed that she had to hold on to the fence again to make her way over to the group, but no one seemed to be paying any attention to her.

"That was fast," Mike commented.

"Sure was," Ashleigh agreed.

Cindy carefully examined the faces around her. They were all cheerful and calm. No one seemed to think anything was wrong.

Honor was still breathing hard. Cindy had never seen her take so long to settle down after a breeze. Honor bumped Cindy with her nose, as if urging her to speak up.

"Honor really seems upset," Cindy ventured.

Jeremy looked surprised. "Maybe a little," he said. "But she'll settle down."

Cindy wondered how he could sound so calm. Didn't he understand that Honor was especially sensitive?

Jeremy smiled at Cindy. "How's it going one-handed?" he asked.

Cindy stared at him, caught off guard. She hadn't expected him to be nice to her. "Not too well," she admitted. "You'd be amazed how much you need both hands to do anything."

"Oh, we've all been there." Jeremy handed Honor's reins to Vic and shrugged. "I broke my wrist a couple of years ago. It took months before I could really flex it again. But don't worry. You'll be okay."

"Thanks." Cindy watched as Jeremy turned to find his next mount. She didn't know what to think. On one hand, she really did believe that Jeremy had ridden Honor too hard. On the other hand, the last time she had been on the filly, she had almost killed her. Cindy sighed. It would be better just to believe that Honor would be fine.

A commotion over by the training barn caught Cindy's attention. Honor and Vic had reached the doorway when, suddenly, Honor reared, striking out. Cindy winced as Vic brought the filly down. She'd never seen Honor strike out like that before.

"Cindy!" Samantha called from the track. "Want to watch me breeze Fleet Street?"

Ordinarily Cindy would have liked nothing more. But she shook her head. "Can't right now!" she called back.

Haltingly Cindy made her way to the training barn, stopping to rest a couple of times. Finally she reached the doorway.

"Hey, Cindy." Vic was sweeping the aisle with a broad broom. He looked surprised to see her. "What are you doing here?"

"I'm going to groom Honor," Cindy said.

"Oh." Vic hesitated for a second. He propped his broom against one of the stall doors. "I already sponged Honor and put her up. Let me get her out for you."

"I can do it." Cindy was already walking toward Honor's stall.

Honor looked over her stall door and restlessly shifted from foot to foot. She still seemed a little wired. The filly's dark eyes were fixed on Cindy, and she bobbed her head.

"I know, you want your grooming," Cindy said. "I guess Jeremy doesn't know that you like to be brushed right after a ride."

Cindy attached a lead line to Honor's halter and led her to a set of crossties. She noted with relief that the fit young filly wasn't breathing hard anymore, and she was completely cool. She seemed to have come out of the workout fine.

With her right hand Cindy clipped first one crosstie, then the other to the filly's halter. "Everything takes me a hundred times as long as it used to," Cindy muttered, opening Honor's tack trunk and removing a body brush.

Honor quivered as Cindy ran the brush over her. "Steady, now," Cindy soothed.

After a few minutes of regular, smooth strokes Cindy could see the filly relaxing. Her ears tipped back, and she rested her weight on three legs. Cindy felt better, too, glad to be doing something useful.

A clatter behind them caused Cindy to jerk her head around. Samantha was bringing in Fleet Street from her exercise. The black filly skittered as her shoes slipped a little on the concrete.

Out of the corner of her eye Cindy saw Honor trying to back away, but the crossties yanked down her head. Squealing with fright, Honor tried to rear, almost losing her balance.

Desperately Cindy reached up for Honor's halter with her left hand. A millisecond later she had to bite down hard on her tongue to keep from screaming. Overwhelmed by pain, Cindy slumped to the floor, dangerously close to Honor's slicing hooves.

"Watch out!" Vic ran toward her. Quickly he hoisted Cindy to her feet and pushed her out of the way.

Cindy fell back onto a bale of hay. She watched unhappily as Vic reached for Honor's head, trying to calm the wild-eyed filly. At last he succeeded in getting Honor to stand quietly, although the filly was still trembling.

Cindy didn't even try to help. No matter how much she wanted to help Honor, she realized that she would only be in the way.

5

"WHAT DID YOU SAY?" CINDY BENT CLOSER TO MAX, A puzzled expression on her face. The beat from the band pounded in Cindy's ears. She could see Max's lips moving, but she couldn't hear a sound over the thump of the music.

Max put his mouth to her ear. "This is a fantastic party!" he yelled.

"Yeah!" Cindy smiled a little. She hadn't really felt much like a party, but she was touched by Heather's efforts. Blue and white streamers fluttered from dozens of the old oak trees at Whitebrook, and a huge buffet had been set out on the lawn next to the McLeans' cottage. There was even a slide show featuring Cindy, the other Whitebrook riders, and their horses, projected onto a big screen Heather had borrowed from the school.

44

"Heather really knocked herself out!" Cindy yelled at Max.

"She had a little help hanging those streamers!" Max said wryly.

The band finished a song and announced a break. The slide show froze on the last slide. Cindy heard groans from the partygoers, but she was glad for a little quiet.

"Let's sit down," Max suggested.

Cindy nodded, but she couldn't help staring at the last slide. It was a huge photo of her and Champion right after the Dubai World Cup. Cindy was looking into the camera with a bright smile, and Champion had his head propped on her shoulder. Suddenly she couldn't bear to look at the oversized evidence of her brief career as a jockey.

Max guided her to a picnic bench. Cindy sat down and tipped back her head. The Saturday evening was cloudy and moonless, and a soft breeze tickled Cindy's face. She sighed.

"Are you hungry?" Max asked. "Want me to get you something?"

Cindy shook her head. "No, thanks."

"Cake?"

"Really, I don't want anything," Cindy protested. "I'm fine."

"No, you're not," Max said gently. "You've looked unhappy all evening. What's the matter?"

"Hey, Cindy!" Sharon Rogers called from the buffet

table. The next moment Sharon, Heather, Melissa Souter, and Laura Billings, with her boyfriend, Jeff Stevenson, were crowded around her and Max.

"Great party," Sharon said. "How are you feeling, Cindy?"

"Not bad." She smiled at her friends. It really was good to see them again.

Samantha turned on a portable CD player next to the bandstand. "Let's dance!" Laura suggested to Jeff.

Dark, muscular Jeff pretended to wince. "Haven't you had enough? We've been dancing for two hours."

"I love to dance!" Laughing, Laura grabbed Jeff's hand and pulled him toward the bandstand.

Cindy watched them enviously, then glanced down at the sling on her arm. It was nearly two weeks after her accident, but her arm still felt almost useless—until she moved it. Then it hurt just as much as ever.

"Do you want to dance?" Max asked as the rest of their friends headed for the dance area.

"No, I don't really feel like it," Cindy lied.

"We could take it easy," Max said. "No wild spins or dips."

Cindy smiled, but she shook her head. She couldn't admit—even to Max—how bad her arm really was.

"You were about to tell me what's been bothering you," Max urged gently.

"Nothing's bothering me," Cindy protested lamely.

"Oh, sure. You've been sighing and frowning all evening," Max said. "Come on—tell me."

"I'm just worried about Honor," she said.

"Why? I heard Ashleigh say earlier tonight that she's happy with how Honor's training is going."

Cindy looked over to where Ashleigh was standing with Mike and Ian. They were laughing about something. They certainly didn't look like they were concerned about Honor's upcoming race.

Cindy hesitated. She didn't want Max to think she was complaining about how Ashleigh and Mike were handling Honor's training. The filly was getting faster and faster, and she was filling out into a magnificent, powerful horse.

"Honor's training isn't going quite right," she said carefully. "I can't put my finger on what it is, though. It's like she's stressed out. I know, I know—" Cindy put up a hand, preventing Max from interrupting. "Your mom's a vet, and we both know that young horses usually are stressed out when they're in training."

"Well, she won't be stressed once you're riding her again," Max said. "She goes best for you; there's no doubt about that."

"But that's the problem. I don't know when I'll be able to ride her again," Cindy whispered. "That's what's really got me down."

Max squeezed her right shoulder. "You've got to hang in there," he said.

The sudden sound of a drumroll interrupted their conversation. "And here he is—the one and only

Dubai World Cup and Triple Crown winner, our Champion!" Ashleigh announced. A spotlight shone to the left of the dance floor.

Suddenly Champion burst into the spotlight behind Ashleigh. The magnificent dark chestnut colt wheeled, his small ears pricked forward. He stopped, sniffing.

"Hey, Champion!" Cindy called, grinning.

Champion stared into the near darkness. Then, with a quick answering whicker, the big colt started toward Cindy, dragging Ashleigh with him. Cindy couldn't help laughing. Champion was one of the most opinionated horses she'd ever known.

Champion marched confidently up to Cindy and nosed her pockets. "Are you up to your old tricks?" Cindy asked fondly, rubbing his ears.

"Here you go, Cindy." Ashleigh handed her Champion's lead rope. "He's all yours."

Cindy smiled. In many ways Champion really was hers. She had loved him and helped train him since he was a foal. Their fantastic win in the Dubai World Cup was just the latest wonderful experience they'd shared.

"I thought I might be seeing you tonight, and look what I brought you, boy." Cindy dug in her pocket for a peppermint, Champion's favorite treat, and unwrapped it for him.

Cindy's friends crowded around as Champion lipped up the treat. "Can I give him one, too?" Heather asked.

"Sure." Cindy handed all her friends a peppermint. Champion worked his way down the line, crunching greedily.

"When are you going to be riding Champion again, Cindy?" Melissa asked.

"Soon," Cindy said shortly. "Mark's riding him for now."

Cindy looked past the bandstand at the tranquil, shadowy paddocks. Suddenly she longed to be away from questions and noise.

"I think I'll take Champion back to the barn," she said quickly. "He's had enough candy for one night."

"Are you sure you can do it?" Max asked.

"I'm sure. You stay and dance a little. I'll be back in a minute." Cindy tugged on Champion's lead. "Come on, boy."

Champion followed her willingly around the crowd and down the path toward the training barn. "At least I can actually make it to the barn this time," she told him.

Champion snorted as if to say, "Big deal." Cindy smiled and rubbed the snip on the end of his nose. Champion might not be very sympathetic, but at least he didn't keep asking her when she was going to ride again.

The moon broke through the clouds, casting a silvery light on Champion's dark coat as Cindy guided the colt through the doorway of the training barn to his stall. She walked him into his stall, then turned to go.

The big colt grabbed the edge of her shirt in his teeth. "Sorry, pal." Cindy laughed, pulling her shirt out of the stallion's mouth. "I have to get back to the party." She gave Champion a final pat.

Cindy headed out of the stallion barn and over to the training barn. She would just check in on Honor before she rejoined her friends.

"Honor?" she called as she entered the dark stable. Usually the moment Honor heard Cindy's voice, she looked out over her stall door.

"Honor?" Cindy repeated softly, looking over the stall door.

The bay filly stood quietly at the back of her stall. At the sound of Cindy's voice she slowly turned her head, but she stayed where she was.

Cindy's heart pounded with fear. This wasn't like Honor at all. She let herself into the stall and approached the filly. "What's the matter, sweetie?"

Tentatively Honor stretched out her nose to Cindy's hand. Carefully Cindy touched Honor's nose, then slowly worked her way up to the filly's head to rub her star. The filly sighed and leaned into the caress.

"You don't so look good." Cindy stepped back to examine Honor. She couldn't see anything wrong. But Honor's stance seemed a little stiff, and clearly she was reluctant to move.

"You're hurting, and you're unhappy." Cindy groaned. "It's no wonder, with Jeremy riding."

Cindy felt helpless. Even though she didn't like the way he rode, Cindy had to admit that she couldn't really fault Jeremy as a jockey. Although he used the whip on Honor, something Cindy had never done, he used it sparingly. And it wasn't his fault that Honor was sore. With Ashleigh, Mike, and Ian overseeing her training, Cindy knew Honor would never be abused or overworked.

Cindy buried her face in the filly's black mane. "Jeremy just doesn't love you like I do," Cindy said softly. "To him, you're just another horse."

Easing her hand down Honor's neck, Cindy gently rubbed the filly's satiny coat. She moved the massage slowly to the filly's sensitive underbelly.

Honor flinched and moved away. Cindy looked at her in surprise.

"What is it, girl?" she asked. Cindy looked underneath the filly and found a small sore where the girth had rubbed. Honor's coat almost hid it, but Cindy could see pink, irritated skin about the size of a dime. "How did that happen?" she wondered. "I'd better put some ointment on it."

Suddenly Cindy felt very tired. She hadn't been on her feet this much since the accident, and the excitement and stress of the party were catching up with her.

Painfully Cindy dragged herself to the medicine cabinet in the tack room. Breathing heavily, she reached for the jar of ointment with her right hand, ignoring the burning ache in her other shoulder that the movement caused. Slowly she walked back to Honor's stall and let herself back in.

Bracing the jar against her leg, Cindy managed to twist off the lid. She put some ointment on her finger and spread it thickly on the sore. "Easy, girl," she soothed.

The filly stood still, as if she knew Cindy was trying to help. Perspiration beaded Cindy's forehead, but at last she had thoroughly coated the sore. She collapsed against the wall and sank down onto the clean shavings. Len, Mark, and the other grooms cleaned out the stalls. But Jeremy was supposed to do Honor's grooming, just like Cindy used to. "He can't be doing it very well if you're getting sores," Cindy said to the filly.

"Cindy?" Max called. "Are you okay?"

Cindy didn't get up. She wasn't sure if she could. "Um, not exactly—I'm in here."

Max's worried face appeared over the stall door. "What happened?"

"Nothing to me." Cindy tried to smile reassuringly.

Max came inside the stall and sat beside her. Honor jumped away in alarm. "What's the matter, girl?" Max asked in surprise.

"That's what I want to know." Cindy filled Max in on Honor's sore and her other problems. "Jeremy's just not treating her right," she finished.

Max was looking at Honor. The filly had calmed down and stood peacefully beside Cindy, occasionally nudging her. The soft barn lights glanced off Honor's shining gold coat, and the ridges of her defined muscles formed pockets of bronze. "Are you sure you're not imagining all this?" Max asked gently.

Cindy took a deep breath. She knew she shouldn't get mad at Max. Honor really did look glorious, not like a mistreated horse at all. "I'm not imagining the saddle sore," she said.

"That's true." Max was silent for a moment. "What are you going to do?"

"Tell Ashleigh. Make a note on Honor's chart. What else can I do?" Cindy shrugged. "I can't ride. I can't even groom her."

Honor nudged Cindy harder and stepped very close, her warm breath tickling Cindy's neck. Cindy's heart went out to her. Honor trusted her, and she seemed to be asking for help in the only way she could.

"Don't worry, sweetheart," Cindy said. "I'll take care of you, no matter what. I promise."

6

"MAYBE I'M NOT READY TO DO THIS." CINDY SAT IN HER mom's car two days later, looking out the window at her school.

"Cindy, you're ready," Beth said firmly. "You've missed enough school. Besides, what would you do at the house all day?"

"See how Honor came out of her exercise this morning," Cindy said quickly. She'd had time to watch the beginning of Honor's workout. The filly had really been full of it, and Jeremy had checked her hard several times. But Cindy had to leave to get ready for school before Jeremy had brought Honor back to the barn. She hadn't been able to see if Jeremy had done Honor any damage.

Beth laughed. "Now that sounds like the *real* reason you don't want to go to school," she said.

Cindy shrugged. "It is. That—and how long it takes me to get dressed," she added in frustration. She'd had to allow extra time to get from the track to the house and struggle into clothes for school: a button-down oxford, loose jeans, which were easier to zip, and loafers.

"At least you're managing by yourself now." Beth sounded optimistic.

"Barely," Cindy muttered. But it was true. By this time she could shower and dress herself, but she had to do everything in slow motion.

"You'll start physical therapy in two weeks if all goes well," Beth said encouragingly. "If you stay busy, the time will fly."

Reluctantly Cindy got out of the car and walked up the path to the school. She was late for first period, and the wide, white halls were empty. Cindy stopped at her locker and took out her books, slamming the tan metal door. It clanged loudly in the quiet.

Leaning back against her locker, Cindy looked up and down the hall. She'd missed only two weeks of school, but she felt like a stranger.

Great. I'm well enough to go to school but not well enough to ride, she thought with a sigh.

Then she straightened her shoulders. She couldn't think that way. She *was* feeling better—and she hadn't had a dizzy spell yet today. "I've just got to be patient," she murmured, starting down the hall toward her English class. "Once I start my physical therapy, I'll be riding in no time. Right now maybe I *should* just concentrate on school."

Quietly Cindy opened the door to her English classroom. Trying not to disturb the class, she walked to her seat.

"Cindy!" Max called. "You made it!" Then, to Cindy's amazement, he began to clap. In seconds the other kids had begun to clap, too. Even the teacher joined in.

Cindy blushed. "Wow, thanks, everybody," she managed to say, sliding into her seat.

"Welcome back, Cindy," Mr. Donovan said. He began his lecture again. Cindy opened her textbook and listened closely. She found that she easily understood what the teacher was saying about a Shakespeare play.

I've got part of my old life back, she thought happily. *That wasn't so hard. I bet the rest of it will come soon, too.*

After school Cindy went straight from the bus to the stable. She was beat after the long day at school, but she wanted to check on Honor's girth sore. It had seemed better last night, since the filly had taken Sunday off from her training. But Cindy hadn't had a chance to look at it this morning after Jeremy had ridden her.

She spotted Honor out in the paddock, grazing

with Fleet Street and Beautiful Music, another black two-year-old filly. Honor stood between the two other fillies, almost rubbing shoulders with them. She was vigorously cropping grass and seemed happy enough.

Cindy smiled and hurried across the paddock to her. Honor looked up with a start at Cindy's approach and moved away uneasily.

"What's the matter now, girl?" Cindy asked, frowning. Honor had never tried to get away from her in the paddock before. The filly usually came right up, expecting petting and treats. "Honor, it's just me—you don't have to be scared!"

Honor stopped after a few paces and lowered her head, but she didn't return to grazing. Her big brown eyes seemed frightened. "This isn't good," Cindy murmured.

Fleet Street bumped Cindy's leg affectionately, and Beautiful Music nibbled her fingers. The other two fillies were acting normally.

Cindy's heart sank. If Fleet Street and Beautiful Music were this relaxed, then nothing had happened to frighten Honor in the paddock. She must have had a bad experience in her morning workout. "Just a minute, you guys," Cindy told the two other inquisitive fillies. "I've got treats for you, but first I have to see what's wrong with Honor."

Her hand outstretched, Cindy slowly approached Honor again. "Come on, girl," she coaxed. "You know I'd never hurt you. Don't be silly."

Honor's small ears pricked, then tipped back, relaxing. Cindy touched Honor's shoulder, then worked her hand up the filly's neck to her head. At last Honor dropped her head to let Cindy reach her star, as if she finally remembered who Cindy was. Cindy sighed with relief.

"Let's take a look at that sore," she said, bending to look under Honor. "It should be better by now, but I just want to make sure." Cindy gasped in shock and drew back. "It's twice as big!"

Cindy leaned against Honor. *How could that happen?* she wondered. Saturday night she'd noted on Honor's chart that the filly had a saddle sore. There was no way Jeremy could have missed the note—he had to look at the chart to see what Ashleigh wanted Honor to do on the track.

Cindy leaned under Honor and looked at the sore again. On Saturday the sore had been dime size, and yesterday it had been half that. Today it was the size of a quarter—and the skin wasn't just pink and irritated; it was rubbed raw and inflamed.

"I guess I should take you back to the barn and call the vet," Cindy told Honor. The filly had resumed grazing and was contentedly cropping the grass in a circle around Cindy's feet. She gazed at Honor, her eyes moving from the proud arch of the filly's neck to the luxuriant black fan of her tail ruffling in the gentle breeze.

"You wouldn't need the vet if Jeremy would just

take care of you," Cindy said, growing angrier by the minute. "I think it's time I said something to Ashleigh about this."

Honor stopped grazing for a moment and looked at her intently, as if to say, "Well, what took you so long?"

Cindy hurried out of the paddock and strode purposefully to the stable office. The barn was still, since all the horses were out in the paddocks, and the office was empty.

Mark and Vic were unloading sacks of grain from a truck and stacking them in the feed room at the end of the barn. "Have you seen Ashleigh?" she asked.

Mark tossed another sack of oats on top of the stack. "I think she's over in the foaling barn with Heavenly Choir," he said. "Heavenly's foal is due any day now."

"Thanks." Cindy knew that spring was always a busy time for Ashleigh and everyone else on the farm, with foals being born, the next breeding seasons for the mares and stallions to book, and Kentucky racing going into high gear. But busy or not, Cindy was sure that Ashleigh would want to hear what was going on with Honor.

Ashleigh was just leading Heavenly Choir back to her big, roomy foaling stall.

Cindy had to smile. "Boy, is she big."

"She sure is. Heavenly's the last mare to foal this year." Ashleigh closed the stall door behind Heavenly

Choir and pushed damp strands of hair off her face. "I think I'll be as glad as she is when it's over."

"Can I talk to you about something?" Cindy asked. She hated to spoil Ashleigh's good mood, but this was important.

"Of course." Ashleigh raised an eyebrow. "What's up?"

"I'm worried about Honor," Cindy began.

Ashleigh held up a hand. "I know, Cindy. But I really think—"

"Wait, you don't know what I'm going to say." Cindy had never had the nerve to interrupt Ashleigh before, but she couldn't stand to hear even one more time how well things were going with Honor. "Honor's got a bad saddle sore," she continued quietly. "I noted it on her chart on Saturday, but today it's much worse."

Ashleigh was silent for a second. "How big is it?" she asked.

Cindy made a circle with her thumb and forefinger. "Like this. But it's bigger than it was on Saturday night." Cindy waited hopefully. She was sure Ashleigh would suggest that they go right out to the paddock and look at Honor.

When she sees what Jeremy's done, maybe she'll get rid of him! Cindy thought.

"Cindy, Honor's probably got very sensitive skin," Ashleigh said reassuringly. "A saddle sore's not the end of the world. I'll definitely take a look at it tonight when she comes in for the evening feeding, and tomorrow we'll try a sheepskin-covered girth on her. But this really isn't a major problem."

Jeremy walked up to them, slapping his crop against his boot. "Hi, guys," he said cheerfully. "What's up?"

"Honor's got a horrible saddle sore," Cindy said. "Didn't you see my note about it?"

Jeremy looked surprised. "Sorry, I didn't," he said. "I talked to Ashleigh this morning about Honor's exercise instead of looking at the chart to see what she should do. I'll watch out for the sore. I don't want Honor hurting when I'm riding—it'll take her mind off running."

"Thanks." Ashleigh smiled, and Cindy could tell she regarded the matter as solved.

"Can I talk to you about something for a second, Ashleigh?" Jeremy asked.

"Sure." Ashleigh and Jeremy walked off toward the office.

Cindy looked after them, her emotions churning. She'd solved Honor's problem—for now. But she was more sure than ever that she had to keep a close eye on Honor, or something terrible would happen to the filly.

7

OVER THE NEXT FEW WEEKS CINDY WATCHED IN FRUSTRA-
tion and growing alarm as Jeremy continued with
Honor's training. Every morning Jeremy groomed
Honor, then took her out to the track. When she was
worked, Honor always put in the top performance of
Whitebrook's two-year-olds, but Cindy could see
how unhappy the filly was. Afterward Jeremy would
hand Honor off to Cindy, who now had enough
energy to groom her. Cindy would try to calm the
bruised, edgy filly, readying her for another day.

One morning in early June, Cindy ran a comb
through Honor's shiny black mane and stepped back
to check her work. In a few minutes Vic or Jeremy
would come by to tack her up, since Cindy still
couldn't use her left arm. Then Jeremy would ride
Honor.

"You look gorgeous," Cindy said with a sigh.

The filly dropped her head and looked at Cindy imploringly, as if to say, "Do I really have to go out there?"

"Yes, you do." Cindy dropped the mane comb into Honor's trunk and gave the filly's neck a reassuring stroke. "I don't like it, either. But there's nothing I can do."

"There's my girl." Jeremy's cheerful voice echoed down the stable aisle. He was carrying Honor's saddle in one hand. With the other he was slapping his crop against his riding boot, the way he always did.

Honor spooked, dancing on her hind legs as far back as the crossties would let her.

Cindy glared at Jeremy's crop, then glanced at Honor with real worry, wondering if the filly was going to rear in the crossties again.

"You're raring to go this morning, aren't you?" Jeremy said with a chuckle. Seeming not to notice anything was wrong, he threw the pad and saddle over Honor's back. Honor shivered and repeatedly tossed her head, but she stayed on the ground.

Cindy stared at Jeremy in amazement, but he didn't seem to notice her expression—or Honor's.

Jeremy swiftly bridled the filly. "Okay, time to go," he said, and led Honor toward the barn door.

Cindy shook her head and followed slowly. School was out for the summer, so she had plenty of time this morning to watch Honor's exercise. But Cindy felt almost as unhappy as Honor. She could hardly stand to watch Jeremy's indifferent treatment of her beloved filly anymore.

Cindy hurried down to the track. The morning sun was already hot, hinting at the steamy summer day ahead. Summer—and the start of Honor's racing career—was nearly here, she realized.

Jeremy and Honor had already reached the gap. Jeremy was talking to Mike and Ashleigh, one boot casually resting on the bottom board of the fence. He nodded at something Ashleigh said, then quickly mounted up and rode off before Cindy could reach them.

"Morning, Cindy," Mike greeted her. "What's new?"

"Nothing much."

"We were just talking about Honor's first race," Ashleigh said with a smile. "The Debutante is only about three weeks away!"

Cindy nodded, trying to smile back. She draped her good arm over the top rail of the fence and stared out at the track. Obviously she was the only one who was worried about whether or not Honor would even make it to her first race.

Jeremy and Honor lapped the track at a slow gallop and continued on into the turn. Cindy watched intently. So far, so good. The filly was galloping with even, fluid strides, keeping the correct distance from the rail. Cindy felt a pang of envy. Jeremy was the one who deserved credit for Honor's businesslike approach to her work.

"They're coming up on the half-mile pole," Mike said excitedly.

"Jeremy's working her a half mile today?" Cindy asked.

"Yep. She should put in her best time yet." Mike stepped onto the track to watch.

Honor had just rounded the turn. The filly's sweeping strides grew longer as she prepared to really run.

Cindy swallowed hard. Ashleigh and Vic had joined Mike on the track. They were all watching Honor with eager expressions.

Cindy tried to watch objectively. She had to admit that Jeremy was a fantastic rider. He sat his mounts easily, with perfect, natural form. Even on the turn he was keeping Honor right at the rail.

"Go!" Cindy whispered as Honor flew by the half-mile pole on the backstretch.

As if she had heard, Honor surged ahead. But the next second Jeremy used the whip hard on her left side.

"What does he think he's doing?" Cindy gasped.

The filly threw up her head in protest and fear. But she was able to gather herself, and her strides became light and free again.

Jeremy whipped Honor again! "Ouch," Cindy cried. "Ashleigh, why is he whipping her?"

Ashleigh didn't look around. To her amazement, Cindy saw that everyone else was beaming.

Honor thundered by, the sound of her hooves that

close up were as deafening as a locomotive. Honor and Jeremy's positions were both perfect again. Jeremy rose over Honor's neck, signaling the end of the ride.

Mike clicked off his stopwatch. "Forty-seven seconds even. Way to go!"

"She's ready for the Debutante." Ashleigh nodded. She turned to Cindy. "Jeremy does ride with a strong hand. But Honor may need that. When Jeremy hit her left-handed, he wasn't being cruel. She was probably too close to the rail. Remember, she ran into the rail with you—she's very strong willed."

"I know." Cindy hung her head. Did Ashleigh doubt her ability to ride Honor? Cindy glanced at her arm, still helpless in the sling—an obvious reminder of Cindy's dangerous misjudgment on the filly.

Jeremy was slowly riding Honor back to the gap. Cindy watched as he dismounted in the middle of the track and led the filly.

Honor stopped, bracing her legs, and shook her head. Her thick mane was soaked, and drops of sweat flew. Then she shuddered from head to toe.

Jeremy backed up to Honor's side and smacked her smartly on the shoulder with the reins. The filly jumped away from the blow and dug in her heels.

"No!" Cindy clutched her head. Jeremy did everything wrong!

Jeremy stepped over to Honor and hit her again.

66

With a sharp snort the filly plunged ahead. Jeremy checked her until he was walking first again.

Honor followed him obediently this time. But Cindy noticed that fresh sweat marks had broken out on her flanks. Honor wasn't cooling down or relaxing at all. In fact, the sensitive filly looked like she was about to fall apart.

Cindy walked toward Honor to take her from Jeremy. At least she could put an end to today's exercise session as soon as possible.

The filly saw her coming and whickered softly, but she didn't walk any faster.

Cindy looked quickly at Honor's legs. She could hardly believe her eyes, but Honor was favoring both of her front feet, jerkily shifting from one to the other. The movement was subtle, but Cindy was sure she wasn't mistaken. "Honor's limping!" she cried in horror.

Cindy ran across the track, barely stopping to check for traffic. If Honor had damaged her legs, her career could be over.

"Get her off the track," Ashleigh said calmly, but Cindy saw her forehead crease with worry. "We'll look at her right here."

Cindy held the reins while Ashleigh gently ran her hands over the filly's legs. Jeremy stood nearby, watching. Cindy noticed he barely looked concerned.

"She's definitely sore," Ashleigh said at last, rising. "We'll x-ray her legs, but I think she just needs rest."

Cindy glared at Jeremy. It was all she could do to keep her temper. Honor needed a rest all right—from him!

"I bet she'll be okay." Jeremy gave Honor a quick pat on the rump, then walked back to the gap.

"Where is he going?" Cindy demanded. Jeremy had so much nerve! Cindy was sure that Honor's shins were sore because Jeremy had whipped her and thrown her off balance, putting too much stress on her legs.

"Jeremy has to ride another horse now." Ashleigh sighed. "Cindy, try not to get too worked up about this. Believe me, we'll watch Honor carefully. I don't want anything to happen to her, either. She's Whitebrook's brightest hope."

Cindy fiddled with the ends of her hair. "Have you thought about my riding Honor again?" she asked.

"Of course," Ashleigh said warmly. "I know you miss that. But Cindy, we all want Honor to do well in her first race, and you're just not going to be ready for it. We'll see what happens—but I want to be fair to Jeremy, too. If he does well, he's entitled to keep going with Honor, at least for a while."

"I'd change the way I rode her if I got to try again," Cindy ventured. "I know I made a mistake the last time. I should have been firmer with her."

Ashleigh squeezed Cindy's shoulder. "I'm not punishing you by taking you off Honor—I'm just being realistic. Why don't you take Honor back to the barn? Len will help you rub down her legs. I'll be there in a minute."

Cindy tugged gently on Honor's reins. "Come on, girl," she said softly. "I'll take good care of you."

Honor touched Cindy's hand with her nose and sniffed. The beautiful filly blew out a huge breath, as if she finally realized her ordeal was over.

"Hey, Cindy!" Max was walking toward her from the McLeans' cottage.

"Hi." Cindy trudged across the stable yard to meet Max. She'd just finished treating Honor's sore legs. "What a great surprise! I wasn't expecting to see you."

"You weren't? But you invited me, remember?" Max said patiently. "We were going to do something today."

Cindy felt her face flush. After she and Max had almost broken up over her obsessive riding schedule when she was preparing for the Dubai Cup, she had promised to make more time for him. But she'd been so worried about Honor lately, it seemed like that was all she could think about.

"Max, I forgot. I'm sorry."

"It's okay," Max said gently. "I didn't have anything special planned."

"Maybe we can just hang out at the house," Cindy

said hopefully. She didn't want to admit to Max how tired she was.

"Actually, your mom mentioned something that just came up that you might be interested in," Max said mysteriously.

"And what's that?" Cindy asked.

"Your doctor just called and he says the X rays of your arm show that the break is healed. You have an appointment with a physical therapist in about an hour."

A huge smile of delight broke across Cindy's face. This was the news she'd been waiting for! Without a moment's hesitation Cindy slid the sling off her arm. "I guess I won't need this anymore," she said triumphantly, flexing her fingers.

But to her dismay, she realized she couldn't even do that very well. Her arm dropped limply to her side, and when she tried to straighten it, she felt a familiar dull ache in her shoulder.

"Are you sure you should have your arm out of the sling?" Max looked worried.

"Maybe I should let the therapist show me how to do it." Cindy adjusted the sling back on her arm. "After this session I want to start riding again."

"I don't know, Cindy." Max hesitated, running a hand through his dark hair. "What's the big rush? Jeremy's riding Honor in the Debutante, isn't he?"

"Not if she can't run at all." Cindy filled Max in on Honor's sore shins.

"She'll probably be fine after a good night's rest," Max said. "She's a strong filly."

"I know, but I'm more worried about her than ever." Cindy was silent for a moment. "Max, do you think I'm way overreacting? Because everyone else does."

"You know Honor best," Max said reassuringly. "And you're not the kind of person who would make things up just to get another jockey off a horse you want to ride."

Cindy frowned. Could Ashleigh interpret her behavior that way? She shook her head. She knew there was reason to worry about Honor. Cindy just hoped it wouldn't take a tragedy to make everyone else see she was right.

"Will you drive me to the therapist?" she asked Max, eager to change the subject.

"At your service." Max took Cindy's hand. "We'd better leave now for your appointment—the therapist is all the way in Lexington."

Cindy got in Max's car and rolled down the window. The day was bright and sunny with a light, warm breeze—a great day to be riding. And now that she was on the way to see the physical therapist, Cindy felt confident she'd be on a horse again in no time.

Max glanced over. "Are you worried about seeing the therapist?" he asked.

"No, why would I be?" Cindy said. "Starting therapy

means I'm really starting to get better—and the sooner I get better, the sooner I start riding Honor again."

"Cindy, you can't plan on riding right away," Max pointed out. "The therapy will take some time."

"But the break is *healed*." Cindy looked out the window again. "And if I start riding right away, maybe I can be ready to ride Honor in her first race if Jeremy screws up."

"That would be great," Max said carefully, turning the car onto the main road. "Let's see what the therapist says."

Max skillfully drove through the traffic once they reached the city and parked in front of a low brick building. "This is it," he said, getting out of the car.

Cindy followed slowly. She didn't want to admit it, but she really *was* a little nervous.

The receptionist smiled at Cindy and Max as they walked over to her desk. "Are you Cindy McLean?"

Cindy nodded. She squeezed Max's hand for reassurance.

"Dr. Kandel is expecting you," she said. "Go through that doorway. He's in the first office on your left."

"You're coming with me, right?" Cindy asked Max.

"I wouldn't miss it for anything," Max said.

Through an open doorway to their right Cindy saw a roomful of exercise machines. In the next room was a big swimming pool. The clean smell of chlorine reached Cindy's nose.

This will be just like going to a health club, Cindy thought with growing confidence as she opened the door to Dr. Kandel's office. The gym in Lexington where Beth taught aerobics looked just like this. The only difference was that the people in the exercise room and pool were all being closely supervised by therapists.

The physical therapist, a blond man in his thirties, rose from behind his desk to greet them. "I'm Dr. Kandel," he said. "Please have a seat while I review your X rays."

Cindy dropped onto the edge of a chair, trying to be patient. She couldn't wait to get started on her exercises.

"Your X rays look good." The therapist examined them with maddening slowness.

"What should I do first?" Cindy asked anxiously.

Dr. Kandel peered at her over his glasses. "Let's start with range-of-motion exercises. Take your arm out of the sling—you won't use that anymore. Lift your arm up as far as you can, then hold it there and count to five."

"Sure," Cindy said eagerly. She slipped her arm out of the sling and handed the sling to Max.

Immediately Cindy lifted her left arm as high as she could. But her arm didn't react the way it had before the accident. It still felt as heavy as lead, and she could barely lift it two inches. Cindy tried to hold it there for a count of five.

"One . . . two . . . ," Cindy said in a quavering voice. Her arm dropped down in front of her before she got to three. "I can still hardly move it!" she cried. "It's supposed to be better by now!"

"Try again," Dr. Kandel said calmly. "Two things are going on with your arm, Cindy—you haven't used it for so long, it's stiff, and the muscles are weak."

Cindy tried again. Her arm began to shake from the effort. She dropped it into her lap on the count of three, tears of pain and fright blurring her eyes. "I can't do it," she whispered.

"Cindy, you have to keep trying," Dr. Kandel urged. "I know it's hard. But if you don't keep exercising your arm, it will stay like that."

Cindy nodded and took a deep breath. Then she lifted her arm again. This time she made it to five.

"Good," the doctor said. "I want you to lift your arm as high as you can every hour, holding it to a count of five. Work on that for a couple of days, then we'll talk about more strenuous exercises."

Cindy nodded again, trying to look confident, but inside she didn't feel good at all. She squeezed her eyes shut, forcing back tears of frustration. She had to keep trying. Honor needed her, and she had to get better before it was too late.

8

"WHY IS THERE A MOVING VAN IN FRONT OF MIKE AND Ashleigh's house?" Samantha asked. She refilled Cindy's orange juice glass and pointed out the window.

Cindy glanced out, too. The morning sun was half hidden behind clouds. A storm front was moving in, and she could see the flowers below the window bobbing in the strong wind. Beyond them a small yellow moving van was parked in front of Ashleigh and Mike's house.

Cindy shrugged and grabbed a bagel from the basket. "The driver's probably lost," she said, pushing her chair back from the table. "I'll go ask him who he's looking for. I was about to head down to the barn, anyway."

With her left hand Cindy picked up a lump of blue Play-Doh from the table. She gave it a squeeze.

"Planning on doing a sculpture of Honor?" Samantha joked.

"Very funny," Cindy replied. "Actually, I'm trying to strengthen my hand."

"Are you doing all your exercises?" Samantha asked seriously.

"I'm doing extra exercises," Cindy said firmly.

"Don't overdo it," Samantha replied. "Your recovery is going to take time. But that's okay, you know—you've got a lot of races ahead of you."

Cindy managed a smile. "I know. I just hope they can be on Honor."

She hurried out the door before Samantha could tell her that Honor was doing great. By now Cindy had given up on trying to convince anyone that the filly was in trouble.

Cindy headed down the driveway and over to the moving van.

The driver was setting up a ramp at the back of the truck. Before Cindy could speak to him, he disappeared inside. A moment later he came back out rolling a dolly with a couple of big boxes loaded on it.

Jeremy walked around the other side of the van. "Hi, Cindy," he said. Then he turned to the driver. "Put the boxes marked bedroom in the front upstairs room," he requested. "All the others can go in the living room for now. Catch you in a bit, Cindy." Jeremy strode off toward the training barn.

Cindy's mouth dropped open in shock. Was Jeremy moving in with Ashleigh and Mike?

She walked slowly to the barn, trying to figure out what that might mean. The wind had gotten even stronger, and her hair whipped in her eyes. Cindy reached for a ponytail holder in her pocket. Then she realized that she couldn't reach behind her head with her left hand to gather her hair into a ponytail. Cindy groaned with frustration.

When she got to the barn, Jeremy already had Honor out of her stall and in crossties. "At least he's spending time with her, even though he can't ride her," Cindy murmured. Since Honor had come up with sore shins, Cindy had worked hard to treat the filly's injuries. Her treatments seemed effective. Last night Honor hadn't seemed sore at all.

Cindy walked to Honor's side, caressing the filly's soft nose. "Hey, sweetheart," she said.

Honor bent her head, sniffing Cindy's hands for carrots. Cindy pulled a big, crisp carrot out of her back pocket and broke it into pieces while Honor fidgeted in anticipation. As Honor lipped the carrot out of her hand, Cindy pictured throwing Honor's saddle on her back, hopping up on the filly, and heading out for a ride. *I wish*, she thought sadly.

"So how's the arm doing?" Jeremy asked.

"Fine," Cindy said shortly.

Jeremy whisked a brush through Honor's tail.

Then, to Cindy's amazement, he reached for the small exercise saddle perched over Honor's stall.

"What are you doing?" Cindy cried. Jeremy had clearly lost his mind. "Honor shouldn't be ridden. She just came up sore yesterday!"

"Well—if Ashleigh or any of the trainers were here, we could ask them their opinion. But they've all gone to an auction." Jeremy flipped the saddle onto Honor's back and tightened the girth. "That leaves me in charge, and I think she needs the work."

Cindy stared at him. "You can't do this!"

"Of course I can. There's nothing to be gained by babying this filly. We've got a big race coming up." Jeremy slipped the bit into Honor's mouth and drew the headpiece over her ears. "See you later."

He led Honor out of the barn. Cindy thought the filly was moving reluctantly. Before turning the corner, Honor turned her head back and stared at Cindy. She seemed to be pleading with her to do something.

Cindy considered her options. Her dad, Mike, and Ashleigh wouldn't be back from the auction for at least another hour. None of the grooms would stand up to Jeremy. As Honor's jockey, it would be expected that he have input into her training. Growing more angry by the second, Cindy realized that there was nothing she could do to stop Jeremy—this time.

"But this doesn't have to happen again," she said aloud. "Not if I can ride Honor."

Cindy stood in doorway Jeremy and Honor had just walked through. Deep in thought, she glanced behind her. Then she realized that Champion was looking straight back at her from his stall. The dark brown colt must have finished his morning exercise, and now he was waiting for someone to take him out to the paddock. From the look on Champion's face, Cindy guessed he thought that person should be her.

"I'll take you out, all right, Champion," she said with sudden resolve. "But not just to the paddock. I'm going to ride you. You're the hardest horse to ride on this farm. If I can ride you, I can ride anyone."

Cindy walked over to Champion and clipped a lead rope to his halter. The colt tossed his head in anticipation and lightly pawed the ground. Cindy hesitated, her hand on the door latch.

"What if I fall?" Cindy worried, running her right hand protectively over her injured arm. She remembered what the doctor had said. If she strained her arm, she could shatter the ball of her shoulder—and only surgery could put it back together.

Champion pulled on the lead rope, obviously not understanding her hesitation. Cindy shook her head to clear it of negative thoughts. She remembered poor Honor, out on the track right now with Jeremy forcing her to run despite her pain.

"I can't let Honor be ruined, no matter what," Cindy murmured. "Okay, Champion," she said with determination. "Let's do this." Cindy opened the stall door and tried to brace herself for Champion's rush out of the stall.

But to her surprise, Champion stepped obediently out of his stall and followed her to a set of crossties.

"Let me just brush you, then we'll get out there on the track," Cindy said. She didn't intend to work Champion hard—he'd already been out that morning. But if she could get him into a nice slow gallop going around the track, Ashleigh was bound to be impressed.

Cindy tossed Champion's brush into his trunk and walked briskly to the tack room to get his saddle. Suddenly she stopped dead. How was she going to get his saddle on with only one hand? She couldn't ask Vic or one of the other grooms to help her, she realized. They would never let her go through with her plan.

"Well, then," Cindy said to Champion. "I guess I'll just have to ride you bareback."

First, though, she'd have to get the bridle on. Cindy dragged a mounting block to the left of Champion's head and stepped up on it. That put her left hand high enough so that she could slip the bit into Champion's mouth without lifting her left arm much. The effort still brought tears to her eyes. Cindy used her right hand to pull the headpiece over Champion's ears.

Champion stood absolutely still. He seemed fascinated by this new method of putting on the bridle.

"That's a good boy." Cindy jumped down from the mounting block and gave him a pat. "Now I just have to figure out how to get on." That would be tricky. Champion was a tall horse, and Cindy had to use a mounting block to get on him even when he was saddled. She would also have to keep her arm nearly stiff as she jumped on his back—or suffer the consequences.

This is crazy, Cindy thought. Her arm was starting to ache already, and she hadn't even tried to ride yet.

"Honor's probably in pain, too," Cindy told herself firmly. "Just figure out what to do."

Leading Champion, Cindy walked slowly up the barn aisle, looking for something tall enough to let her climb onto Champion's back. Her eye fell on the extra-large tack trunk in front of Champion's stall.

Cindy glanced around to see if anyone was watching, but luckily no one was in sight. She shut Champion's stall door so the colt wouldn't try to get back in, then lined Champion up with the trunk. "Come on, move over, boy," she said with a grunt, pushing against his right side.

When Champion was as close to the tack trunk as she could get him, Cindy slid the reins over his head and climbed onto the top of the trunk. She gripped a handful of Champion's mane tightly in her right hand. "Stand still, boy," she whispered. She was going to have to try to get her right leg as far over Champion's back as she could and then sort of wriggle into place on his back.

Champion wasn't making things easy. He knew something different was going on, and the big colt was squirming with excitement.

"Champion, for once in your life, behave," Cindy said through gritted teeth. Normally she loved the spirited colt's antics. But Cindy knew that if Champion wasn't an angel today, she wouldn't be able to handle him.

Best Pal, Cindy's tortoiseshell cat and Champion's special friend, paused in the aisle and stared at Champion. The colt stopped fidgeting and bent his head to sniff the cat.

This may be my only chance to get on—now! Cindy thought, and jumped high out over Champion's back. She landed heavily, nearly sliding down the colt's strong neck.

Champion spooked at the sudden weight on his back, tossed his head up, and almost threw Cindy off sideways into the wall. Instinctively Cindy tried to grab his neck to balance herself, but her left arm was nearly useless. She almost screamed from the awful pain.

Quickly Cindy sat up, instinctively squeezing her legs tight in preparation for Champion's next move, but her weakened muscles barely kept her upright. Sensing his advantage, Champion clattered out of the barn at a trot. Cindy lost her balance. She fell forward, her good arm around the colt's neck.

"Champion, walk!" Cindy begged, but the colt

ignored her. He quickened his trot, heading in the direction of the paddock.

Cindy could feel herself slipping off to the left. She made a last grab at Champion's mane, but the colt's bouncing gait unseated her more with every stride. *There's no way I can stay on*, she realized. *Oh, no—what have I done?*

At the last second Cindy twisted and took the impact of the fall on her right side. Her head hit the ground. "Ow!" Cindy cried. In an instant she sat up, although her head was reeling. She had to get hold of the reins again. If Champion got away from her, things would only get worse.

To her surprise, Champion stood right next to her. Cindy had expected him to run off to the paddock, but the big colt just dropped his head to look at her, as if he couldn't figure out what was going on. She reached out for his reins in a daze.

"Cindy, sweetheart!" Suddenly her dad was kneeling beside her, a frightened expression on his face. "Let's get you to the hospital right away."

"No, I don't need to go to the hospital!" Cindy cried, even though her arm hurt almost as much as it had the day she first injured it. Looking up, she saw Ashleigh and Mike standing next to her dad. *Why did they have to come back just in time to see this?* Cindy thought unhappily.

"What on earth did you think you were doing?" Mike asked incredulously.

"Nothing I'll ever do again." Cindy wiped away her tears of pain and humiliation. She saw Jeremy riding Honor over from the track, probably to see what the commotion was about.

"Cindy, you're in no shape to ride," Ashleigh said firmly.

"I know that now." Gripping her dad's arm, Cindy managed to get up. "And I don't think I ever will be."

"Don't say that—" Ashleigh began.

Cindy turned toward the house. "I'll never be able to ride anything but a pleasure horse," she said sadly. "Maybe not even that."

"You haven't been doing your exercises," Dr. Kandel said to Cindy two days later, leaning back in his chair.

Max glanced at Cindy but said nothing. He'd offered to drive her to her appointment, and Cindy had gladly accepted. She just had to get away from her family. Since her fall from Champion, her mom and dad hadn't let up, insisting that she rest and take it easy. Cindy couldn't stand the fuss. To make things worse, Honor seemed to be okay, and that made her ride on Champion seem even more crazy.

She studied the therapist's diplomas on the wall and shrugged. "Those exercises hurt too much," she said flatly. "I don't want to do them anymore." Cindy hadn't tried to lift a finger of her left hand since her fall. Now Dr. Kandel was making her do her range-of-motion exercises. Cindy was doing worse than she had the first day she'd tried them.

"Be glad the exercises do hurt," the therapist said sternly. "Once your arm stops hurting, that will mean it's as well as it's ever going to be."

Cindy felt a icy shiver run down her spine. But she just shrugged again. "I'm not improving anyway," she said.

"Of course you are," the therapist argued. "Or you were—until you stopped doing your exercises."

"So what?" Cindy cried. "Why should I suffer like this? After all those exercises I could get my arm halfway to my head. Big deal! I can't ride. I'll never ride again!"

"You must miss that," Dr. Kandel said softly. "You're a jockey, I know. I saw you ride in the Dubai World Cup."

Cindy remembered those intense seconds of speed in Dubai as she and Champion took on the finest horses in the world. She remembered the roar of the crowd, and her unbelievable joy in Champion's victory. "I was a jockey," she said unhappily. "But I'm not anymore."

Tears blurred Cindy's eyes. "The day before yesterday I fell off that horse I rode in Dubai. I couldn't handle him at all. My career as a jockey is finished."

"Cindy, you can't just give up," Max urged. "I know you can ride again."

Cindy shook her head. "I'm not so sure."

85

"Do you really want to give up riding without making an effort to get better?" Dr. Kandel asked her.

"You always believe in the horses, Cindy," Max said. "This time you have to believe in yourself."

Cindy realized that Max was right. It hadn't been easy to win in Dubai, but she had always believed Champion could do it. Deep down, she knew those moments of glory in Dubai were the results of months of hard work and dedication.

"You're right," she said finally. "I have to try—for me . . . and for Honor."

"All right!" Max said enthusiastically.

"I'm not encouraging you to do anything foolish, Cindy," the therapist warned. "Don't start off with the most challenging racehorse in the barn. And listen to what your body is telling you—don't keep going if you're in severe pain."

"I'll work up to riding the racehorses," Cindy agreed. *But I won't give up on my dream to ride Honor to victory,* she promised herself.

9

Later that afternoon Cindy went down to the paddock to get out Chips, the Appaloosa exercise horse that she often let her friends ride.

"Here, Chips!" Cindy called. "Apples!"

The Appaloosa jerked up his head and stared at her with his wild-looking, white-rimmed eyes. Cindy walked quickly to his side before Chips realized she had come out to catch him. The gelding stepped sideways, but Cindy quickly held out an apple. Chips hesitated, then bit into it.

"I know you were having fun out here," Cindy said, buckling on the halter. "But what I want to do is much more important than eating, even though I know you don't think so."

Chips snorted loudly, but he followed Cindy obediently to the gate. *I hope nobody sees us*, she thought, crosstying Chips in the barn. Cindy wanted to make sure she could put in a good ride before she had an audience.

"This I'll time do it right," she told herself. Chips twisted his head to look at her. "I know, I know—you don't see what the big deal is about going for a ride." Cindy patted his splotchy neck. "But I need to think for a minute."

Cindy walked to the tack room and looked around. The racehorses' and retired racehorses' saddles hung on pegs in neat rows. "Ashleigh's Wonder, March to Glory, Wonder's Champion." Cindy read aloud the names of the great champions at Whitebrook. With one finger she gently touched Wonder's saddle.

Cindy sighed and stepped to the other side of the room, where the exercise horses' tack was kept. "What would help me stay on?" she murmured, looking around the tack room. Cindy took down a bridle with a pelham bit. She knew Chips would probably go fine in a snaffle, but she couldn't take any chances. Besides, with a stronger bit she wouldn't have to pull as hard on the reins.

"Riding bareback was definitely not a good idea with Champion," she murmured, lifting a hunt seat saddle off the wall. That saddle, with its deeper seat and knee rolls, would give her much more support than the tiny, flat exercise and racing saddles.

"Okay. I think I'm set." Cindy drew a deep breath

and carried her tack back to Chips. She couldn't help feeling nervous.

Cindy threw the saddle over Chips's back and groped under his belly for the girth. Using just the fingers of her left hand, she was able to buckle the girth while drawing it tight with her right hand.

Chips stood perfectly still while she struggled. "Good boy," Cindy said gratefully. Unlike Champion, Chips always tried to help his rider.

Using a mounting block, she put the bridle on him the same way she had with Champion. Then, leading Chips, she moved the mounting block to the doorway of the barn. "Here goes," she said.

Chips again stood still, and Cindy had no problem getting her left foot into the stirrup. She balanced herself with her right hand on Chips's neck and swung her right leg over the saddle. "That's it!" she said under her breath.

The Appaloosa set off at a steady walk around the stable yard. "I'm riding!" Cindy said with growing excitement. She extended her left arm over Chips's neck. The effort made it shake, but the pain was bearable. *All right!* Cindy cheered mentally. *I'm ready for my comeback.*

Ashleigh was walking out of the stallions' barn. Cindy sat up straighter, looking to make sure her left arm was where it should be. Then she asked Chips to turn. The Appaloosa obligingly made several big loops.

"Hey, you're doing well, Cindy," Ashleigh commented. "It's wonderful to see you back on a horse again."

"It feels great, too." Cindy did a tighter loop with Chips to prove she had control of him.

"Very nice," Ashleigh said approvingly.

Cindy stopped Chips and looked appealingly at the older jockey. "I really feel fine," she said. "Can't I try riding Honor?"

Ashleigh looked troubled. Cindy felt her hopes sink. "I mean, I could just exercise her," she stammered. "Maybe . . . maybe just walk her around the track, or even the stable yard."

Ashleigh exhaled sharply. "Cindy, I'm sorry. I know how much you want to ride Honor, but right now I think we should stick with one rider on her. Jeremy's been working with her for a month. If we changed riders now, we'd risk exciting or confusing her even more."

"But if she's already excited and confused . . . ," Cindy began hesitantly. "Don't you think changing riders might help?"

"There are two problems with that." Ashleigh stepped over to Chips's side and absently rubbed the gelding's nose. "First, there is a big difference between riding Chips and riding Honor. She's a lot like Champion—headstrong and excitable, and she needs a very firm hand. I don't want you to get hurt again."

"I'm willing to risk it. Just let me try once!" Cindy begged.

"Cindy, I'm sorry," Ashleigh said gently. "Even if you somehow got well enough to ride Honor this summer, I've made a deal with the Townsends and Jeremy—he gets to ride Honor in her first race."

Cindy's heart sank. Jeremy was going to ride Honor in her first race, and that was that.

"Just keep up the good work," Ashleigh said encouragingly. "You'll be back on the racehorses soon."

Cindy nodded, turning Chips away so Ashleigh wouldn't see the tears sliding down her cheeks. There was nothing she could do to help Honor now.

"Would someone get the phone?" Cindy called from her room. She really wasn't in the mood to talk to anyone. She'd been sitting on her bed, staring at the photos of her on Champion and wondering if she would ever ride a racehorse again. The phone continued to ring. With a sigh, Cindy picked up the phone next to her bed. "Hello?"

"Are you ready?" Max asked.

"Ready for what?" Cindy had no idea what he was talking about.

"Ready for the tenth-grade pool party," Max said. "It's today, remember?"

"Oh, yeah."

"I'll be over in a few minutes," Max said. "Okay?"

"I guess." Cindy felt too depressed to go to a party. "Maybe I should just stay here and play with Kevin and Christina in their pool," she joked half-heartedly. "Theirs is only a foot deep—I could probably handle it."

"Dr. Kandel told you to keep up with other exercise," Max said firmly. "So we're going."

"All right." Cindy groaned. Max sounded determined enough for the both of them.

"Okay. Be right there." Max hung up.

Cindy gathered her swimsuit, towel, and sunscreen and went downstairs to tell Beth she was leaving. Beth sat in a low chair on the patio next to the aboveground plastic pool. The moment Christina and Kevin saw Cindy, both children stopped splashing each other and waved.

"Stay with us!" Christina said brightly.

Cindy smiled at the little girl. "I'll swim with you tomorrow. Right now I have to meet Max for a pool party with big kids."

"Boo," Kevin said, taking aim at her with a squirt gun.

"Hey, no fair!" Cindy protested, backing away. "I'm unarmed. You just wait till tomorrow." Kevin laughed.

Beth smiled wryly at Cindy and pointed to her own wet hair. "As you can see, I already lost the battle. Have fun at your party."

"I will." Cindy heard Max's car pulling up in the driveway. She dashed through the house, grabbing a horse magazine off the kitchen table as she went.

Max leaned over the front seat and opened the passenger door for her. "This really is a cool car," Cindy remarked, sliding in. Max had bought his car, an almost new black Mustang, just a few months before.

"Gee, thanks." Max shook his head. "I don't know how you can stand not knowing how to drive."

"Why should I learn to drive when I've got you?" Cindy teased. "No, seriously, I went out driving with Sammy a couple of times last week. She said I wasn't too dangerous. Now that it's summer, I should have more time to practice." *And since I'm not riding in races, I probably have time for all those things I never did before,* she added to herself with a grimace.

Max looked over at her. "What?" he asked.

"Oh, just the whole deal with me riding." Cindy shrugged her good shoulder. "For one thing, it's just so frustrating that no one will listen to me. But even worse is that nothing can stop Jeremy from riding Honor in her first race now."

"Do you still think it'll turn out that badly?" Max asked seriously.

"I don't know. Maybe not." Cindy stared out the window. The day was perfect for a pool party—hot and humid, with lots of sunshine—but Cindy was barely aware of it. "I just feel like Honor's on the edge, and it wouldn't take much to push her over."

"And nobody else sees it? That's a little hard to believe," Max commented.

Cindy frowned. "I know it is! I can only see it because I know her so well. If I could just ride her around the stable yard, I bet that would help calm her down." Cindy picked at the fluff on her towel. "It doesn't really matter anyway. Ashleigh won't replace Jeremy as Honor's jockey now—the Debutante's coming up in just three weeks."

Max parked in the community pool parking lot. "I guess all you can do is hope for the best."

"Yeah." *And try to be with Honor as much as possible,* Cindy added to herself, feeling a stab of guilt over spending the afternoon at the pool.

"Hi, Cindy. Hey, Max!" Heather called from the high dive.

"Hey!" Cindy sat down on a chaise and slipped off her street clothes and sandals. Moments later she waded into the shallow end of the pool.

The water was cool and refreshing. Cindy ducked underwater and came up, smoothing back her wet hair. Max dove in from the side of the pool and swam over to her. "I wish I could dive," Cindy said wistfully.

"Maybe you can," Max suggested.

"I don't think so." Cindy watched Heather, Laura, and some of her other friends line up at the high dive.

"You could show me your exercises," Max said, playfully splashing her.

Cindy rubbed the water out of her eyes. "Here? Give me a break!"

"C'mon," Max persisted. "I want to see what kind of progress you're making."

"If you promise not to bug me for the rest of the day . . . ," Cindy said.

"Promise." Max grinned.

Cindy began her series of movements. She was amazed by how easy it seemed to let the water lift up her arm. "Hey, this is great," she admitted.

Max stood to the side, a huge smile on his face as he watched Cindy go through her exercises with growing enthusiasm.

"Cindy! Max! Want to play water polo?" Jeff called from the side of the pool.

"Okay!" Cindy and Max smiled at each other.

Soon a spirited game of water polo began. Cindy swam slowly after the beach ball, trying to get close enough to hit it into the other team's goal. Zack Laffrey, a friend of Max's, beat her to it and took a shot. Cindy hung back, waiting to see if he'd make it.

Suddenly she realized she'd drifted into the deep end of the pool. Automatically she started treading water. "Max, look!" she shouted. "I'm treading water! I never thought I could move my arm this much."

"Way to go!" Heather called from the other team.

Cindy forgot her arm as she swam from one end of

the pool to the other, chasing the ball. She was right in front of the other team's goal—and Max passed her the ball, high in the air. Without thinking, Cindy batted it down with her left hand. The ball flew into the goal. "Yes, yes, yes!" she yelled.

"All right!" Max cheered.

"No, not the goal." Cindy swam over to him. "That's the highest I've been able to lift my arm since the accident!"

"Good going." Max slapped her a high five.

They played for about another hour. Finally Heather called, "Who wants to go to the snack bar?"

"We do!" Cindy and Max said in unison.

Cindy walked up the steps out of the pool to her lounge chair. She sat down, shaking water out of her hair, and picked up her towel. "Who won?" she asked Max breathlessly.

"I have no idea." Max laughed. "Let's get something to eat."

"I'll be there in a minute." Cindy waved, then walked to the edge of the pool. She sat on the side of the pool with her legs in the water. Small waves lapped over her knees, and the afternoon sun was losing a little of its strength. For the first time since the accident, she felt hopeful. She *was* getting better. Now if she could just figure out how to help Honor . . .

10

CINDY WALKED DOWN THE DIM BARN AISLE TO THE FILLY'S stall. Honor stood with her head over the webbing at the front. Under the barn night-lights her dark eyes were big and luminous, and she eagerly arched her sleek, golden neck as she waited for Cindy to come closer.

Honor had been in the barn at Churchill Downs for a week, working on the track where she would run her first race. Cindy had tried to come over to the track every day and spend as much time as possible with the filly. Finally it was the night before Honor's first race.

Honor pushed at her softly with her nose, and Cindy rubbed her cheek against the young horse's satiny coat. "You miss me, don't you," she whispered. "I'm the only one who can tell you're not happy."

Honor's clockings had been good in her two works this week on the Churchill Downs track. But she'd almost run out on Jeremy after the last work, the fastest of her career. Cindy had overheard Jeremy say something about how Honor thought she could get away with misbehaving like that—after what had happened with Cindy.

Cindy clenched her fists just remembering. *How dare he?* she fumed. Honor had run into the rail with Cindy because Honor was young and had made a mistake. Cindy was willing to admit that she'd made one, too—she hadn't kept the filly well enough in hand. But she was sure that Honor had almost run out on Jeremy because she had panicked, trying desperately to get away from Jeremy and his relentless jerks on the bit, stinging whip, and stern voice.

"How about I stay in the stall with you tonight, Honor?" Cindy asked. "You'd like that, wouldn't you? Then you'll be in a good mood for tomorrow."

Honor's ears flicked into a relaxed position. Cindy rubbed the filly's neck with long, soft strokes.

"I don't think it's such a good idea for you to spend the night in Honor's stall," Jeremy said.

Cindy looked around, startled. Jeremy and Ashleigh stood right behind her. Honor jerked up her head, then stepped to the back of her stall. "Why not?" Cindy asked. "I always stayed with Glory and Champion when I thought they really needed me. . . ."

Jeremy frowned. "That's my point—Honor *doesn't* need you in the stall for any reason I can think of. She's not used to people sleeping in her stall. It's a new factor, and I don't want to add one right before her big race tomorrow."

Cindy looked quickly at Ashleigh. The decision was really up to her. Cindy was sure Ashleigh would side with her on this one. After all, this had nothing to do with riding. This was a question of who knew Honor best—Cindy or Jeremy.

Ashleigh hesitated and looked uncomfortable. "Jeremy may be right. Let's not test out a theory now, the night before Honor's first race."

Cindy felt totally betrayed. But she could tell from Ashleigh's expression that there was no point in arguing. "I'll . . . just say good night to Honor, then," she stammered.

"Of course you can say good night to her, Cindy," Ashleigh said understandingly.

"Catch you two later." Jeremy gave an offhand wave. "I'm going to get some sleep."

Ashleigh nodded. "See you tomorrow."

Cindy looked over the top of Honor's stall door. "Come here, sweetie," she said. The filly walked right over and dropped her head on Cindy's shoulder. She huffed out a little sigh of contentment. Cindy closed her eyes, trying not to fall apart herself.

"Cindy, I know how you feel about staying with Honor—and you may be right," Ashleigh said. "But I can't upset Jeremy right now, either, by not taking his advice. He and Honor are a team, and I've got to try to keep them together."

Cindy sighed deeply. She knew that Ashleigh believed she was doing the right thing—for everyone involved. "Well, you don't mind if I stay here for a little while with her, do you?" Cindy ventured.

Ashleigh smiled. "Not at all, Cindy. I'm not trying to be harsh. And clearly Honor loves having you around—that has to be good for her."

Cindy managed a smile. "Same for me."

"I'm going back to the motel in a little while," Ashleigh said. "But your dad's still here—he can give you a ride back. I'll tell him to come find you before he leaves."

Even though Whitebrook was only fifty miles away, Cindy, her dad, Ashleigh, and Mike were staying in a motel close to the track. They wanted to be at the barn early on race day.

"Okay. See you tomorrow." Cindy watched Ashleigh leave, then turned back to Honor. Picking up a brush from the top of Honor's trunk, Cindy let herself into the stall. She felt better just being close to her beloved filly. "I've never seen a prettier horse than you, but we've got to get that straw off."

Cindy began to brush Honor with soothing strokes. "Don't worry, sweetie," she murmured. "I'll be here first thing tomorrow. There's no way I'm going to leave you alone on your big day."

*   *   *

The sun had barely crept over the horizon when Cindy got to the track the next morning. She decided to check in with Honor first thing.

As she headed toward the filly's stall, Cindy saw Jeremy approaching from the other end of the barn. Cindy increased her pace, hurrying toward the stall. Jeremy did, too, almost as if it were a contest between the two of them. Panting slightly from the exertion, Cindy arrived at the stall a step before Jeremy.

Honor poked her head out the door and whinnied. Cindy was glad that Honor stayed at the front of the stall even when Jeremy walked up. *Maybe she's in a good mood today*, Cindy hoped.

"How's it going, Cindy?" Jeremy glanced at the clipboard he was carrying. "You're here early."

"Yeah, I am." Cindy didn't want to say any more. She didn't want to give Jeremy the impression that she didn't trust him.

She glanced sideways and studied Jeremy as he made a note on his clipboard. Much as she disliked him, she had to admit that he'd always been polite and professional with her. *He treats me the same way he does Honor*, Cindy realized suddenly. *He deals with me just as much as he has to, nothing more. To him this is all just another job.*

Cindy decided to walk out to the track and watch the morning exercise sessions for a little while. She'd go back and spend more time with Honor when Jeremy had left. "See you later," Cindy said, giving Honor's black nose a pat.

"Okay." Jeremy didn't look up.

Cindy walked slowly to the track, her sneakers stirring up small clouds of dust. Cindy knew she had a long day ahead of her—the Debutante didn't go off until about four that afternoon.

She stepped up to the fence and looked around the track. The sun had fully risen, a red ball shimmering through the early morning mist. The horses on the track seemed to melt into the dusty sunlight.

A coal black horse thundered down the stretch, his jockey crouched low over his neck. The colt's black coat looked like burning embers in the red light.

Cindy unconsciously leaned farther out over the fence, as if she were riding with them. "I just wish I could get out there," she murmured longingly.

"Morning, Cindy." Ian walked up behind her and rested a hand on her shoulder. Ashleigh was right behind him.

"Hi, Dad. Ashleigh." Cindy didn't take her eyes off the colt.

"He's a beauty, isn't he?" her dad asked. "That's Shining Comet."

"His sister, Comet's Journey, is running against Honor this afternoon in the Debutante," Ashleigh said.

"Hmmm." Cindy looked at the colt with renewed

interest. Like Honor, all the fillies entered in the Debutante boasted fine pedigrees. This would be their first race—and the first indication if they had the potential to become champion racehorses.

"Seen enough?" Ashleigh asked. "I want to go check on how Honor's doing."

Cindy nodded, and she and Ashleigh quickly made their way to the backside. As they approached the stall, Cindy could see that Honor was restless. "What's the matter, girl?" Cindy stepped inside the stall. Streaks of sweat darkened the filly's coat. "She wasn't hot when I checked on her earlier."

"Well, it's a hot day." Ashleigh didn't seem concerned. "And of course she's probably excited about the race."

Cindy thought briefly about telling Ashleigh that Jeremy had been to see the filly earlier that morning as well. But she knew it wouldn't do any good. Ashleigh would only think Cindy was being paranoid.

"I'm going to sponge her off," Cindy said, letting herself out of the stall.

"Good idea." Ashleigh wiped her forehead with her hand. "Whew, it's going to be a scorcher."

"Sure is," Cindy agreed. "You should probably go rest somewhere cool. It's going to be a long day."

"I think I'll take that advice," Ashleigh said. "I'll be back to check on Honor later."

Cindy filled a bucket with cool water. Taking a

large sponge from Honor's tack trunk, she began wiping down the filly's sweaty coat. Soon Honor seemed much more comfortable. She stopped pacing and sweating and seemed content to stand quietly.

"It's almost time to take Honor to the saddling paddock." Mike's face appeared over the stall door.

Cindy looked up from her book. She was reading in a corner of Honor's stall. "We're ready," she said.

"I'll say." Mike looked admiringly at the filly. Cindy had brushed her until her sleek coat was a sweeping blaze of gold and her black stockings gleamed like silk.

"Do you want me to take her?" Mike asked.

Cindy shook her head. "That's okay."

Honor followed Cindy obediently on the long walk from the backside to the saddling paddock, where Ashleigh and Ian joined them. "Hold her steady," Ashleigh cautioned.

"I will." Cindy had no intention of moving from Honor's head. The filly seemed to have suddenly realized what was planned for her. She danced on her hindquarters, trying to see the fillies in the other stalls. "Settle down, girl," Cindy soothed. "Save it for the race."

"She's trying to get a look at the competition," Ian joked.

Cindy tried to smile, but she didn't feel so good

anymore. She'd hoped that Honor's tranquil mood would last until she got on the track.

Honor squealed as Ian rested the tiny racing saddle on her back. "Watch her, Cindy," Ashleigh warned.

Cindy moved even closer to Honor's head, trying to get the young horse's attention.

"The other fillies are upset, too," Ashleigh said. "They're all just babies."

Cindy kept her attention on Honor. The filly's dark eyes rolled, and she nervously stamped her hoof, but she stayed on the ground. "Good girl," Cindy breathed. "Can I take her around the walking ring now?"

Ashleigh nodded. "Keep her moving. That way she won't have time to think too much."

Cindy quickly took Honor around the walking ring, where a crowd had gathered to look at the horses.

"There's Honor Bright," she overheard an older man saying. "What a beauty. She's really got the look of her grandam, Ashleigh's Wonder."

Cindy managed a smile, but Honor was tossing her head so hard that even with her good arm Cindy was having trouble keeping her under control.

She led Honor over to where Jeremy was waiting to mount up and handed him the reins. "Thanks, Cindy," he said. "We're all set."

Cindy just nodded. She felt a lump in her throat as Ian gave Jeremy a leg into the saddle. Honor's neck and flanks were darkened with sweat, and flecks of foam had appeared around her bit.

"The rail is really slow today," Ashleigh said.

"I'll watch out for that. We're in the five position, so we should be able to stay clear of the rail." Jeremy gathered his reins.

"Good luck," Cindy ran her hand lightly along Honor's shining neck, then let it drop.

"Thanks." Jeremy turned Honor toward the tunnel to the track.

"Let's go watch from the stands," Ashleigh said cheerfully.

"Sure." Cindy put on a smile. No one was going to accuse her of being a spoilsport.

Beth and Kevin were already sitting in the stands. Beth waved, and Kevin jumped up and down. "Cindy!" he called. "Over here!"

Cindy made her way along the aisle to Kevin and gathered the little boy into her lap. "We'll watch the race together," she said.

"The fillies are going to the gate," Ian announced, focusing his binoculars.

Cindy reached around Kevin to adjust her own binoculars. Honor was at the head of the pack, marching toward the gate, which was positioned at about the middle of the backstretch for the five-and-a-half-furlong race.

"Honor's going into the gate nicely," Ashleigh said.

Cindy could feel her shoulders relax just a little. Maybe Honor would do okay after all.

"The horses are in the gate," the announcer called. "And they're off!"

Cindy quickly moved her binoculars, searching for Honor. The eight fillies were so far away, for a moment she saw only a jumble of black, brown, and gray bodies. Then she saw a bright bay flash as Honor moved quickly to the lead. "Go, girl!" Cindy screamed.

"Honor's showing sharp speed!" Ian called excitedly.

"Look at her go!" Beth agreed.

Cindy saw Jeremy cock his right arm and gasped. "Why is he going to whip her?"

The next moment Jeremy's whip hit Honor's right shoulder hard. The filly sprang forward as if she'd been stung.

"What's he doing?" Ashleigh cried. "She's going plenty fast."

"Maybe Jeremy's just trying to get her attention," Ian said, but he looked tense.

He got it, all right. Cindy almost twisted her program in two. She could tell that Honor hadn't understood the reason for the whipping, either. The filly had gone faster for a stride or two, but now she had fallen off the pace a little.

"Tell her what to do, Jeremy!" Cindy muttered frantically.

"And it's Honor Bright by one; back two to Comet's Journey. So It Ain't Said is third, with Far Cry running in fourth . . . ," the announcer called.

The field of fillies pounded into the turn, a blur of churning dirt and flying hooves. Honor was still holding her lead, but Comet's Journey was creeping up on her. Jeremy lifted his whip again in his right hand.

Before he could strike her, Honor darted inside, crossing several lanes of the track. "Oh, my God—what's she doing? She's going into the rail!" Cindy cried. Mike half rose from his seat.

But Honor stopped her headlong plunge and straightened out, almost skimming the rail.

"Get her away from there, Jeremy!" Ashleigh cried. "The track's too slow at the rail today."

"But that's where Honor thinks she should be! She's moving away from the whip." Cindy stared at the track, willing Honor to move away from the rail.

"He's trying to get her away, but she isn't responding." Ian dropped his binoculars and groaned.

"She doesn't understand!" Cindy could have wept. Jeremy was hauling on Honor's mouth instead of whipping her. But Honor continued to run on the deep, slow surface near the rail.

"What's wrong, Jeremy?" Ashleigh said under her breath. "Get her away from the rail and moving! There's no time for misunderstandings in a race this short."

"Comet's Journey is enjoying a very easy trip just behind the leader," the announcer said.

Cindy and Ashleigh exchanged worried looks. Even if Honor managed to hold on to her lead, Comet's Journey might still have the energy to contend at the finish.

The field pounded around the turn, heading for home. Now Cindy could see Honor clearly. She was only half a length in the lead over Comet. The valiant filly was digging in deep, but Cindy could see she was struggling.

"Here comes Comet!" Ashleigh cried. The black filly had switched leads and with a new burst of power roared up on Honor's outside.

Honor's ears flicked back, as if she were asking Jeremy for help. The filly was sweating freely and looked exhausted. Cindy could almost feel how confused, tense, and tired the young horse must be. Jeremy lifted his whip.

"Oh, no," Cindy groaned. A second later Honor dropped off the pace again, as if she finally couldn't take any more. The wire flashed overhead.

"And Comet's Journey runs down Honor Bright in the final sixteenth of a mile to win!" the announcer called.

Cindy handed Kevin to Beth and rushed out of the stands, pushing between people to get to the track as fast as she could. She had to make sure Honor was all right.

Jeremy and Honor had almost reached the gap.

Honor was trotting, jerking her head up with every stride. Her lovely golden coat was lathered and so dark with sweat, it matched her black stockings.

"Oh, girl." Cindy went quickly to her head and rubbed her wet neck. "Second place isn't so bad! I know you did your best. This wasn't your fault."

Jeremy dismounted and handed Honor's reins to Cindy. "She needs a good cooling out," he said matter-of-factly.

"She sure does." Angry as she was, Cindy decided not to say anything more. She'd never gotten anywhere arguing with Jeremy. "Come on, sweetheart," she said to Honor. "Let's get you back to the barn."

"How is she?" Ashleigh asked, walking up to Honor.

"Okay, I think—just really hot," Cindy replied tersely.

Ashleigh nodded, looking relieved. She turned to Jeremy. "What happened out there?" she asked. Ashleigh sounded more stunned than angry.

Jeremy frowned. "The filly got rank on me, and I couldn't get her out of that hole near the rail."

"You whipped her right toward the rail," Ashleigh pointed out. "She's very sensitive and overreacted."

"If she's that sensitive, maybe you should find another rider," Jeremy said calmly.

"I think I should," Ashleigh agreed.

"What's going on here?" said a loud, angry voice. Turning, Cindy saw a well-dressed young blond woman striding toward them.

"Oh, no, not Lavinia!" Cindy muttered.

110

"Really, Ashleigh, I don't think you have any business insulting my cousin," Lavinia sputtered.

"There was no insult intended." Ashleigh shrugged.

"We had a deal that Jeremy was to ride Honor," Lavinia insisted. "She's our horse, too."

Cindy shook her head. "Come on, Honor." Cindy couldn't believe Lavinia hadn't even looked at Honor to see how she had come out of her race. The filly's head hung dejectedly, and she was still breathing in ragged gasps. Honor followed Cindy docilely toward the backside.

A moment later Cindy heard quick footsteps behind her and turned to see Ashleigh.

"That's it for Jeremy, no matter what Lavinia threatens," Ashleigh said with finality. "I'm sorry, Cindy—you were right. I should have seen long ago that Jeremy wasn't the right rider for Honor."

"At least he's gone now." Cindy grimaced. She could still hear Lavinia talking loudly to somebody.

Ashleigh looked sadly at Honor. "At this point I don't think we should race Honor for the rest of the season, or at least until fall. We need to go back to the beginning with her. Poor girl." Ashleigh rubbed the filly's damp shoulder.

"I don't know if putting her out to pasture would be a good idea," Cindy said timidly. Maybe Ashleigh was finally ready to listen to what she had to say about Honor. "I don't think she'll forget her bad experience that way."

"So what do you suggest?" Ashleigh raised her eyebrows.

Cindy hesitated. "Honor probably wouldn't tolerate another new rider now. I could ride her—"

"But Cindy," Ashleigh began. "She'd be even harder to control now than she was before your accident. . . ."

"Not if I do take her back to the beginning—and me too," Cindy said quickly. "I'll take it really easy with her, just walk her and trot her until we're sure of each other. Then we can go on from there." *And win a race*, Cindy added to herself.

Ashleigh looked serious. "Cindy, I'll have to think about it. This time I really want to do what's right for the filly—and for you, too."

"When will you be done thinking?" Cindy asked eagerly.

Ashleigh looked from Cindy to the exhausted filly and back to Cindy again. "I'll watch you ride Honor tomorrow afternoon, then make my decision."

11

CINDY'S STOMACH WAS IN KNOTS AS SHE WALKED TOWARD the training barn. In half an hour Ashleigh would meet her in the stable yard to watch her ride Honor. Ashleigh had asked her just to walk the filly, but Cindy knew that this was a momentous ride anyway—for both of them.

For a second she hesitated outside the barn, sniffing the sweet scent of the sun-warmed purple and white lilacs surrounding the barn. The day was drowsy and hot, with the soft drone of bees in the flowers and the wind ruffling the long grass. School had been out for a month, but Cindy really hadn't felt like she'd been on any kind of a vacation. Today she would find out if this was going to be the best summer of her life—or the worst.

Honor had been vanned home from the track that

morning. At first she had been a bit skittish and excitable, but they had turned her out to graze in the warm sun, and Cindy expected that by now the filly would be full of grass and contented.

As she approached the barn, Cindy could see a crowd gathered in front of Honor's stall: Ian, Mike, Len, Vic, and the other grooms. Honor was looking out of her stall, as if she were waiting for Cindy, too.

Cindy gulped. "Okay, everybody," she said, with more confidence than she felt. "Let me get Honor out."

"We'll go get front-row seats." Mark touched Cindy's arm. "No, seriously, if we make you nervous, we don't have to watch."

"It's okay. I guess I've had people watch me ride before," Cindy said. But somehow she was more nervous now than she was before a big race. "Here we go," she said, taking a deep breath.

Cindy slid open Honor's stall door and slipped a halter on her. The gorgeous horse pranced eagerly out of the stall.

Cindy looked at Honor and sighed. "I really hope this isn't a disaster," she whispered.

Honor put her head down and nosed Cindy's pockets, looking for treats. When she didn't find any, she pushed her head against Cindy's leg, asking to be scratched. As Cindy rubbed the sensitive spot behind Honor's ears, the filly let out a snort of pleasure. "You still trust me, don't you girl?" Cindy murmured. "We'll be fine."

Cindy picked up a body brush and slowly rotated her arm, trying to work out the stiffness that settled in it if she didn't move it for a while.

She gave Honor a quick brushing. The filly didn't really need a grooming; Len had done that when he had brought her up from the paddock. But Cindy felt like she needed to follow the routine she and Honor used to have.

Putting away the brush, Cindy slowly and patiently began to get Honor tacked up. By now she could move her arm well enough to do almost anything. Her physical therapy had strengthened the muscles, and her therapist was hopeful she would regain full use of her arm.

Cindy took Honor's saddle from on top of her tack trunk. Honor shifted her weight nervously as Cindy eased the saddle onto her back and tightened the girth. Taking the bridle off the hook near Honor's stall, Cindy moved up to Honor's head.

Honor tried to avoid the bridle, sticking her nose as high in the air as the crossties would permit. Cindy waited patiently until the filly dropped her head, then pulled the headpiece over her ears.

Cindy checked her tack carefully, postponing the time when she would have to lead Honor out into the stable yard and mount up. This one ride meant so much. She had to convince her dad and Ashleigh that her arm was just as good as it was before the accident—and that she could control Honor.

"Be good for me, sweetie," Cindy whispered as she led Honor to the barn door.

Cindy and Honor crossed the stable yard. Her dad was leaning against the fence surrounding the yard, his arms folded across his chest, frowning. Vic, Philip, and Mark sat on the top board of the fence. Len stood next to them. He gave Cindy a wink. Ashleigh was next to Mike, smiling encouragingly.

Honor followed her to the mounting block but skittered her hindquarters away as Cindy climbed up the steps.

For a moment Cindy considered trying to jump on Honor the second the filly's fidgeting brought her close enough to the block. But that hadn't worked with Champion, and she doubted it would work now. Cindy knew she had to get to the bottom of Honor's fears, not ignore them. She jumped off the mounting block and walked close to the nervous filly.

"It's okay, girl," she said softly, patting Honor's shoulder. Cindy waited until Honor stood quietly, her ears flicked back in response. Working quickly but with no sudden movements, Cindy led her back to the mounting block and swung into the saddle. She smiled broadly. *I'm back,* she thought.

The bay filly tossed her head and broke into a nervous, jigging trot. Cindy quickly focused her full attention on Honor. She couldn't afford to forget that

Honor had had some bad experiences with her riders lately.

Honor shivered, looking around. "It's just me, girl," Cindy said gently. "Easy does it. Just a walk for me."

The filly dragged against the reins, trying to trot. Cindy gritted her teeth as her left arm began to shake from the strain of holding the strong young horse. "You're not like Chips, are you?" she asked, trying to calm Honor's nerves with her voice. "This may be even harder than riding Champion."

Talking steadily, Cindy guided Honor around the stable yard. The filly minded, but unwillingly, Cindy noticed unhappily. She was taking corners sloppily and trying to dart across the yard. "Don't act like you did with Jeremy," she whispered.

For just a moment Honor seemed to hear. The unbearable pressure on the reins stopped, and the filly's walk became less jarring. "That's the way," Cindy said, blinking back tears that had filled her eyes.

Ashleigh lifted her hand, signaling Cindy to stop.

"Okay, that's enough for the first day, girl," Cindy said soothingly. *That's enough for me, too,* she thought, trying not to grimace with pain. She looked hopefully at Ashleigh, praying that she couldn't tell how much the ride had hurt.

"Did we do okay?" she asked.

Ashleigh nodded. "Well enough to keep going with

her. Your dad agrees. We'll see how she comes along, just taking one step at a time. Good job, Cindy."

"Thanks!" Cindy said happily. She dropped her cheek to the filly's mane and hugged her around the neck. "We're a team again, girl," she whispered. "But we've got a lot of work to do before you can race."

For the next several days Cindy rode Honor regularly, every afternoon, but only at a walk. That was partly for her own sake—even Chips's slow, ambling trot jarred Cindy's shoulder badly if she did it for long. But she also wanted Honor to relax at the slow pace, to learn again to trust her rider and enjoy the ride.

"How's she doing?" Max asked late one afternoon, leaning over the paddock fence.

"Great." Cindy stopped Honor at the far side of the paddock, then asked her to walk on. The beautiful filly obediently moved off in a sprightly but measured walk.

"Why are you riding Honor in the paddock?" Max asked.

"Because she likes it out here." Cindy had decided to ride Honor in the paddock sometimes just to reinforce the idea that being ridden was a pleasant, nonthreatening experience. So far, her theory seemed to be working.

Max pointed at the stormy sky. "Are you coming in?"

"I guess so." Cindy squinted up regretfully. Fat raindrops had just started to fall. "I want to trot her once around first," she added. "Want to watch? It's the first time I've tried it with her since the accident. Tell me how we look."

"Sure." Max climbed up on the bottom board of the fence to see better.

Cindy repositioned her feet in the stirrups of the small, flat exercise saddle. Although the exercise saddle didn't provide as secure a seat as the hunt seat saddle she'd been using, Cindy had decided that she was babying herself too much. She wanted to be ready when she was back in a racing saddle. "Okay, girl—trot!" she said, urging the filly forward with a squeeze of her legs.

Honor broke into a high-speed, rattling trot. Cindy almost groaned aloud as the bouncing gait jarred her shoulder again and again. Doggedly she made several circuits of the paddock. By the last trip Honor was moving at a steady, much smoother pace.

"That's enough," Cindy gasped.

Breathless, she stopped Honor at the gate and pushed her wet bangs off her forehead. The rain was really coming down now. "Did I look off balance?" she asked Max.

Max shook his head. "You looked good," he said. "Really good."

"Thanks. I only hope Ashleigh agrees." Cindy slumped back in the saddle, wishing the pounding in her shoulder would ease up just a little. "I want to move Honor ahead in her training. I'm going to try to gallop her in a week or two."

"Are you ready for that?" Max asked.

"Yeah, she's really coming along." Cindy had to smile at Honor, patiently flicking raindrops off her ears as she stood in the warm summer rain. "It's funny—" Cindy began thoughtfully.

"What's funny?" Max leaned over the fence and took Honor's reins so that Cindy could dismount.

"There are two ways you can ride Honor," Cindy said, looking at the ground. It looked awfully far away. She was in no hurry to dismount because it would make her arm hurt even more. "She can either be forced to mind—that's what Jeremy tried to do— or she can want to please."

"Why don't you come inside?" Max urged. "We can talk some more in the barn."

"Okay." Gray-black clouds swept across the sky, scattering rain across the deep green paddocks. Cindy quickly slid to the ground, trying not to move her left arm, but the pain made her gasp as tears sprang to her eyes.

"That hurt a lot, didn't it?" Max asked.

"Yeah, kind of." On top of the fresh jarring sensation Cindy could still feel the thud of Honor's trot pulsating in her arm.

"Would it help if I rubbed your shoulder?" Max asked sympathetically.

120

"That would be nice." Cindy managed to smile. Max was being very sweet, and she appreciated all the nice things he'd done for her since her accident. But she didn't want to tell him that she doubted a massage would do her arm any good. The pain was in the bone.

That night Cindy arranged a heating pack on her shoulder and settled into her pillows to sleep. "Tomorrow I'll try trotting again with Honor," she said to herself, wincing as her shoulder moved a little off the pillow. "She did so well today."

Cindy picked up a novel in her right hand and began to read. She already knew from experience that if she could just relax, the pain would be less.

But she couldn't seem to relax tonight. The throbbing in her arm only reminded her of how hard she'd had to work just to trot Honor. "I'm so far from getting her back to the racetrack," she said aloud.

Cindy dropped the book and groaned. Her arm really hurt. "Maybe I should take an aspirin," she murmured. But she hated to do that. Her therapist and doctor had advised against it. "If you're in constant pain, that's a sign you're overdoing," Dr. Kandel had said.

But she didn't have any choice. If she didn't get Honor back on track with her training, the talented two-year-old would waste her first racing season.

Cindy had to do what was best for Honor, no matter what the consequences

Gingerly Cindy slid her shoulder off the pillow. "Maybe I shouldn't elevate it," she decided.

She closed her eyes, trying to visualize beautiful things to take her mind off her pain: the horses running from the storm in the paddocks this afternoon, their manes and tails blowing wildly in the strong wind; Max's sweet words of encouragement. But the pounding in her shoulder wouldn't go away.

"Okay, I'll take an aspirin," she told herself, swinging her legs over the side of the bed.

She headed down the dark hall to the bathroom and opened the medicine cabinet. The phone rang as Cindy was struggling with the childproof cap on the aspirin bottle. She rushed back to her room and grabbed the phone off her night table. "Hello?" she said breathlessly.

"Hi, Cindy, it's me," Ashleigh answered. "I just wanted to see how you were doing."

"Not too bad," Cindy lied.

"Really? I saw you riding Honor in the storm, and it's still damp out. I've been injured a couple of times, and the pain was always worst in wet weather."

"Well, my arm does kind of hurt," Cindy admitted. "But don't worry," she added quickly. "It's not so bad that I can't ride."

"Cindy, I'm on your side," Ashleigh said. "I'm not

looking for an excuse to take you off Honor. I can't believe what a difference you've made already. I know you're making sacrifices. I wanted to tell you I appreciate it—and I know Honor does, too."

"Thanks." Cindy sat down on her bed. Just hearing Ashleigh's words made her feel better. "So what was your worst injury?" she asked.

"Probably the time I fell off a claimer at Turfway," Ashleigh said. "That was a long time ago. I had to wear a neck brace for weeks, and I looked like a spaceman."

Cindy giggled. "Yeah, I have to hold my arm so stiff, sometimes I feel like a robot."

"The timing of my injury was awful, though," Ashleigh said. "I really needed to ride Fleet Goddess to get her ready for her first race."

"So what did you do?" Cindy lay on her back, staring at the ceiling.

"Luckily Sammy was able to exercise ride her for me," Ashleigh replied. "Or I should say, she wasn't allowed to, but she did anyway. Finally, after your dad and Sammy didn't speak to each other for a week, he relented."

"That's a great story," Cindy said.

"You've got it tougher than I did because I had help." Ashleigh was silent for a moment. "Anyway, for what it's worth, here's how I've handled pain: Try not to fight it. And don't be scared."

"I'll try." Cindy smiled. She already felt better.

Ashleigh was talking to her jockey-to-jockey, assuming that Cindy would come through it just like she had.

"Good," Ashleigh said. "That's all you can ever do—try your hardest and believe in yourself."

"Thanks for calling," Cindy said drowsily. "You've helped a lot more than an aspirin would have."

"Anytime," Ashleigh replied. "And Cindy?"

"Yes?" Cindy pulled her sheet up around her and clicked off her bedside light. She knew she'd be asleep in minutes.

"Just one more thing—don't give up, ever."

12

CINDY LED HONOR OUT TO THE STABLE YARD FOR THEIR daily ride. She paused to let a pair of mallard ducks cross her and Honor's path. The plump, green-necked male and his brown-speckled female lived on one of Whitebrook's ponds and had taken to walking around the grounds every morning.

"Foolish ducks are going to get stepped on one of these days," Len grumbled from the doorway of the training barn. Len was always complaining about the ducks and often spent part of his morning trying to chase them back to the pond.

"Let them be." Vic stood next to Len in the doorway. He grinned. "They add atmosphere to the place."

Honor looked dubiously at the waddling, quacking ducks. "Oh, Honor, don't be a baby," Cindy said, urging the filly forward. Honor stamped her foot and snorted at the retreating pair. "I can see you take Len's side." Cindy laughed.

Honor stared after the ducks for another few seconds, then, with a toss of her mane, followed Cindy confidently.

Ashleigh walked out of the training barn, leading Beautiful Music. "I have a question for you, Cindy," she said. "How do you think Honor would do on our track?"

"I don't know," Cindy said honestly. She'd wondered that herself recently. A week ago she'd risked taking Honor out of the paddock onto the trails. The filly had gone beautifully, even at a gallop, and Cindy's arm had hardly hurt at all. There was no doubt in Cindy's mind that Honor had a lot of confidence in her again. It was as if their accident had never happened.

Cindy studied the filly. Honor stood quietly, as if she were enjoying the cool, sweet-smelling morning. She briefly touched noses with Beautiful Music. The black and the gold filly were friends who were often put out to pasture together.

Taking Honor out to the track so soon might undo all their hard work, and Cindy was a little nervous about being back on the track herself. It would be the first time since her accident. *But she's a racehorse, and I'm a jockey. The track's where we belong.* Cindy squared her shoulders and turned to Ashleigh. "There's only one way to find out how she'll do."

Ashleigh nodded. "That's what I thought. She looks ready—are you?"

Cindy swallowed hard. What if Honor tried to run out? What if she fell again?

Ashleigh seemed to notice her hesitation. "It was just an idea," she said, turning Beautiful Music to take her out to the track. "We don't have to rush into anything."

"Wait." Cindy couldn't bear to be left behind. "We really are ready." She positioned the mounting block and swung into the saddle.

"Great." Ashleigh turned and smiled. "We'll take it easy."

Cindy concentrated on breathing slowly and deeply, trying not to communicate her nervousness to the filly. Honor was eagerly following Beautiful Music, but Cindy doubted if Honor had figured out yet where they were going.

The July day was hot and humid, and the far side of the track seemed to be melting in a blue haze as the horses and riders approached the gap.

"Take Honor around at a walk and a trot," Ashleigh said when they reached the track.

"Okay. Come on, Honor," Cindy said. The filly was walking very slowly up the slight hill to the track. Suddenly Honor stopped dead at the gap, bracing her legs and pinning her ears.

"Come on, girl," Cindy whispered. "Remember all our great rides? This is going to be another one, I promise."

Honor hesitated, but her ears finally relaxed and

she moved out onto the track. "There you go," Cindy said with relief. "Just walk, girl, while we get used to this again." Honor settled into a brisk, easy walk at the rail.

Cindy smiled, sitting to Honor's comfortable movements. When she wasn't upset, the filly had wonderfully smooth gaits. Almost without being asked, Honor glided into a quick, floating trot. The filly seemed to accept that this was just another ride and obeyed perfectly. Cindy circled the track twice with Honor, then looked to Ashleigh for instructions.

"Go ahead, try her at a gallop," Ashleigh called.

"Okay." But Cindy hesitated. Would Honor be harder to control now, after all her bad experiences?

"Are you all right?" Ashleigh asked.

"Yep." Cindy leaned forward slightly, asking Honor for a faster trot. "I'll gallop her when we get to the backstretch!" she called back.

The beautiful filly glided around the first turn, her black mane and tail glittering in the sun. As she moved into the stretch her pace increased. "You know, don't you?" Cindy asked softly. She shook her head, concentrating only on what they were about to do. Cindy crouched over the filly's neck and let up on her reins just a little.

Honor exploded into a gallop, burning across the track. Cindy let her run a couple of strides, then checked her with the reins. Her heart was pounding. What if the filly didn't slow down?

Honor slowed in response to the pressure on the reins, but to Cindy's alarm she veered toward the rail. "Not too close!" Cindy said, firmly pulling on her right rein.

The filly responded, moving to just the right distance from the rail. Cindy gasped with relief. "Steady, girl," she whispered, not letting her attention waver for a second. "Just keep it up."

Honor stayed at a slow gallop, but Cindy could feel the filly's uncertainty. She tested Cindy's grip on the reins, first drifting in toward the rail, then drifting back out. Cindy's left arm shook from the strain of holding the filly steady, and her shoulder hurt so much, she had to bite her lip to keep from crying out.

"Honor, just go back close to the rail the way you're supposed to," Cindy begged. She glanced at the rail, then down to Honor's pounding hooves. The rail and ground were a flashing blur at racing speed, close to forty miles an hour.

Honor rounded the far turn, staying right where she should on the rail. Her effortless gallop ate up the ground, and Cindy felt herself go with the movement. Despite the pain in her arm, a big grin stole across Cindy's face. "We're ready to race again!" she said joyfully.

At the gap Cindy pulled up the filly and guided her over toward Ashleigh. Honor pranced, lifting each hoof high, as if she knew just how well she had done. Hardly daring to breathe, Cindy waited for Ashleigh's response.

"Excellent, Cindy." Ashleigh was beaming as she walked up beside Honor. "I think she's back!"

Cindy screwed up her courage. "Back enough to race?" she asked.

Ashleigh looked thoughtful. "Maybe," she said. "I was considering the Magnolia at Ellis Park, on August ninth. That would give us just over three weeks to get ready."

"The Magnolia's six furlongs, right? I'm pretty sure I could have her ready for that," Cindy said eagerly.

Ashleigh nodded. "I think you're Honor's only hope—I don't want to try anyone else as jockey after what she's been through." Ashleigh looked Cindy in the eye. "Are you up to riding her in the race?"

"Yes," Cindy said immediately, forcing herself not to rub her aching shoulder.

Ashleigh frowned. "Racing could be dangerous for you. I absolutely don't want you to get hurt again, Cindy."

"I'll be fine," Cindy insisted. Honor was standing quietly, switching at flies with her tail, as if to assure Ashleigh that she'd behave herself.

"Okay," Ashleigh said. "You still have some work to do. I noticed that Honor was drifting out. Probably your left arm is still weaker than your right, and so you're applying more pressure to the bit with your right."

Cindy nodded, but she wasn't so worried anymore. If Ashleigh knew that Cindy's arm was weak but still thought she could ride, that was a plus. Besides, in three weeks Cindy expected to be even stronger than she was now.

"It's decided, then. We'll point Honor toward the Magnolia," Ashleigh said. "It can't hurt. Let's pick up tomorrow with another slow gallop and keep working with her here for the next couple of weeks. Then we'll van her over to Ellis Park a week before the race to get her used to the track."

"Sounds good." But Cindy groaned inwardly at the thought of galloping Honor again so soon. She'd hoped to have a day off to recuperate.

Before she could think about it anymore, Cindy quickly dismounted, keeping her back to Ashleigh so that she wouldn't see her grimace of pain when she hit the ground. Cindy put up her stirrups and reached for Honor's reins.

Honor twisted around swiftly and grabbed a mouthful of Cindy's T-shirt. "Honor, quit it!" Cindy cried.

The filly instantly let go. There was no mistaking the look of pure glee in the Honor's dark eyes.

"Did Champion teach her that?" Ashleigh asked with a smile.

"Maybe. She is kind of like him." Cindy looked closely at Honor. "She's got his spirit, and she's strong."

"All Wonder's offspring and great-offspring have that spirit," Ashleigh said. "Wonder's an amazing horse."

Cindy smiled as Honor lipped at her back pocket, reminding her that it was carrot time. She knew Honor was going to be amazing, too.

"I don't want to break our date, but I'm not really sure I should go to the movies," Cindy said to Max that evening over the phone. She was dead tired after her strenuous gallop on Honor, and it was only six-thirty. The movie started at eight, and Cindy was sure that by then she'd be snoring.

Cindy sat up on her bed, trying to shake off her fuzzy sleepiness. The truth was, she had forgotten about the movie entirely.

"Why don't you want to go?" Max asked.

"Oh, it's been kind of a long day." Cindy rubbed her eyes and nervously gripped the phone. She didn't want Max to start nagging her about riding too hard.

"Are you all right?" Max sounded concerned.

"Yeah, I'm fine." Cindy had finally taken some aspirin, and now the aches in her arm were just a dull throb. "Just tired," she added.

"Well, I guess you should get some sleep, then." Max sounded so disappointed that Cindy felt bad.

"You know what? I've changed my mind. A movie actually sounds pretty good," she said quickly. "It'd be good for me to think about something besides horses. And I really want to see you."

"Great," Max said cheerfully. "I'll come pick you up in fifteen minutes, okay?"

"Okay." Cindy clicked off the phone and rushed to her bureau to get out a clean shirt.

She got dressed in comfortable black jeans and the Churchill Downs T-shirt Heather had gotten her. The shirt was big, but Cindy thought she looked sort of cute in it. And she knew that Heather would be pleased to see her wearing it.

A few minutes later she heard the sound of Max's car on the gravel drive. Cindy ran a brush through her hair, then hurried down the hallway and downstairs.

Her dad, who was reading the newspaper in the living room, looked up. "Don't be late," he said. "You and Honor are in training."

"Isn't it great?" Cindy said cautiously. Ashleigh had already talked to Ian about Honor running in the Magnolia with Cindy as jockey. Her father had given his permission, but Cindy could see from his expression that he wasn't too thrilled.

"It's great if you're sensible about it." Her dad frowned. "I made an appointment with your orthopedist for tomorrow. I want to make sure you're not rushing this."

Cindy rolled her eyes. She knew perfectly well she was rushing it—nobody knew better than she did that her arm wasn't healed. "Well—I feel good!" she said brightly.

Her dad smiled. "You look very pretty, sweetheart. Have a good time."

"I will." Cindy opened the door just as Max was lifting his hand to knock. "Hi," she said.

"Ready to go?" Max asked. "Heather's waiting in the car."

"Is she still acting like a widow?" Cindy took Max's hand, suddenly glad she had decided to go out.

Max laughed. "Yeah, Doug's still gone." Heather had been seeing Doug Mellinger since last spring, but Doug was spending the summer working on his grandfather's ranch in Colorado.

Max squeezed Cindy's hand, and Cindy smiled up at him. Max bent to give her a quick kiss.

Heather rolled down her window in the backseat. "Hey, you two, are you going to be doing that all night? If you are, I'm outta here."

"No, we'll hold back, at least until we're in the dark theater." Cindy grinned and ran around to the front passenger door. Max started the car, and Cindy turned around to talk to Heather.

"I really, really miss Doug." Heather sighed.

"He'll be back in about a month, right?" Cindy asked.

"I guess, if he doesn't stay in the Wild West." Heather shrugged. "He loves it out there—riding mustangs across the desert and hanging out with the cowboys. He gets up at four every morning."

"He probably doesn't like that too well," Max said.

"Oh, you know Doug—he's a really hard worker. Like you, Cindy."

"I guess." Cindy yawned. The long day was catching up with her again.

At the movie theater Laura and Jeff and Sharon and her boyfriend, Rich Farrell, were waiting at the ticket office. "Let's go in," Jeff said impatiently. "Where were you guys?"

"Waking up Cindy." Max joked.

"Doesn't look like you succeeded," Laura laughed.

"Nope." Cindy yawned again.

"Come on—let's get seats." Max took Cindy's hand.

In the movie theater Cindy leaned back in the comfortable seat. They'd missed the coming attractions, and the movie was about to start.

"What's it about?" she whispered to Heather, who sat next to her.

"Ireland," Heather whispered back. "In the nineteenth century."

Images on screen of green, misty hills and slapping ocean waves rolled through Cindy's tired mind. "It's so pretty in Ireland," she murmured, closing her eyes as the mournful strain of violins filled her ears. "The music's nice, too."

"Yeah," Heather said, sounding very far away.

*　　*　　*

135

"Cindy?" Max shook her right arm. "Hey, are you there?"

"What?" Cindy opened her eyes. The movie theater was lit up, and the last few people were waiting to get out the doors. She sat bolt upright in her seat. "Is the movie over?" she asked groggily.

"Yep." Max pulled her to her feet.

"The movie was good, wasn't it?" she said as Max led her up the aisle. "All about Ireland . . . "

Max laughed. "Actually, Cindy, it was about aliens. They took over the world, and a big green one was riding Honor."

Cindy smiled sheepishly. "I guess I don't really know what most of the movie was about. But I remember the beginning."

"Why are you so beat?" Max asked. "You've been riding Honor for weeks. What's different about today?"

Cindy stopped and looked at him carefully to see if he was mad. He didn't seem to be—just curious. "I rode a lot today," she said.

"I *know* that," Max said patiently. "But you're not usually a total zombie afterward. Did Honor act up."

Cindy shook her head. "Just the opposite. Ashleigh wants to enter Honor in a race, with me riding."

Max stared at her in surprise. "Why didn't you tell me? That's big news."

"Because . . ." Cindy hesitated. "I think Honor's ready, but I'm not sure I am."

"Why—are you in a lot of pain?" Max frowned.

Cindy raised her left arm. It was so stiff, she couldn't get it higher than her waist. She closed her eyes as the old dull, throbbing ache began. "Some," she admitted. "But it doesn't matter. All I have to do is make it through race day."

"In one piece," Max added. "Come on, we'd better get out of here. I think they're about to lock the doors."

"Where are we going?" Cindy asked. "Where'd Heather and everybody go?"

"Out to eat." Max opened the car door for her. "I told them to go ahead and order—that we'd be along as soon as I zapped you with a thousand volts or something."

Cindy groaned. She hesitated before she got in the car. "Am I an awful girlfriend?" she asked.

"Nope." Max took her in his arms and kissed her forehead. "You're brave, and stubborn, and determined. I love you the way you are."

"And I feel the same about you," Cindy whispered just before Max's lips met hers in a soft kiss. Max pulled back and looked at her. Smiling tenderly, Cindy entwined her hands behind his neck, tilting her face for another kiss. It was funny, but suddenly she didn't feel sleepy anymore.

13

"Doesn't it feel good to be back?" Cindy asked Honor as she led the filly out of the shedrow at Ellis Park. Two weeks of hard training had flown past. Now Cindy was about to work Honor for the first time on the track where she would race in the Magnolia.

And in just one week Honor would run the most important race of her life.

Honor pranced at her side, nipping her back pockets. Cindy grinned and pulled out a carrot. "You're the prettiest girl at this whole track," she said proudly, stroking Honor's neck.

Honor tossed her head, her black forelock spilling over her perfect star, as if to say that she certainly did know how pretty she was.

Cindy looped Honor's reins over her arm and retied her ponytail, noting with relief that she could actually do it. The early sun, spilling down in cracks through the clouds, was already warm on her face and neck, and the backside was bustling with activity. Horses headed out to the track with their exercise riders, and grooms were busy caring for their horses after workouts. In the wash area a bay colt sighed with enjoyment as warm water sluiced over his steaming sides.

Magic Wand, a cocoa-colored filly, was walking behind a groom, her body wet where the saddle pad had been. Magic Wand was considered to be Honor's main competition in the Magnolia. Cindy wondered if the filly had worked and if so, what her time had been.

Cindy sighed contentedly. She loved all the confusion and excitement of the busy backside.

"You sure you're up for this?" Mark asked, walking up to Cindy with Beautiful Music. Ashleigh wanted to gallop the two fillies together.

Cindy nodded confidently. Dr. Martin, Cindy's orthopedist, hadn't been happy about letting her ride, but after giving her about a million warnings he'd agreed to sign the release. The track doctor had been even harder to convince. He'd said he wanted to watch her ride today.

Cindy flexed her shoulder. Good—no pain. She was sure the track doctor would pass her after today's ride.

"Then let's go!" Mark said, smiling.

Ian walked over to Cindy from the shedrow. With a quick, practiced movement he gave Cindy a leg up into the saddle, then put Mark up. "Okay, you both know what to do," he said. "Keep the fillies well in hand. Don't play killer out there. Just take them for an easy gallop, then work them a half mile."

Cindy nodded. She wasn't worried about Honor going after Beautiful Music, her good friend.

"Good luck." Ian stepped away from Beautiful Music, and Honor followed the black filly onto the track. Mark pulled Beautiful Music up at the gap, and Honor stopped beside her stablemate, her ears pricked forward with interest.

"Let them get their bearings," Mark suggested.

Cindy looked across the track. The sun, still low in the sky, cast a soft glow across the dirt track. Horses and riders were getting in their early workouts, some walking or trotting near the outside rail, others galloping toward the inside of the track. A gray filly roared across the finish line, her rider crouched flat over her neck, her gray-and-black mane streaming behind her.

"Let's get out there!" Cindy said, suddenly impatient.

"Right behind you," Mark replied. They walked the horses out onto the track, keeping to the outside rail for their warm-ups.

Cindy spotted the track's doctor at the finish line,

his eyes glued to her. She knew he intended to watch her for any sign that she wasn't fit to ride.

Shifting a bit in the saddle, Cindy rotated her arm. She asked Honor for a trot, and the filly moved off lightly. Cindy posted easily to the motion as they moved just ahead of Beautiful Music.

Cindy put all thoughts out of her head except those of this ride. "Let's see how you do running against another filly," she said, patting Honor's shining neck. In the week since Honor had been at the track, Cindy had galloped her in company, twice with Beautiful Music and once with the black filly and one of Whitebrook's claimers. Honor had behaved perfectly, but an easy gallop was much different from moving at racing speeds.

Honor lapped the track next to Beautiful Music, trotting in step with the other filly as if they were circus horses. "Ready to gallop?" Mark asked.

Cindy glanced behind them on the track. No other horses were close. "Okay," she said. "Go, Honor!"

The filly instantly shifted into the higher gear, her black hooves easily churning across the track. Cindy went with her, leaning over Honor's golden neck, her hands buried in the filly's black mane.

Beautiful Music was galloping steadily at Honor's flank. They were approaching the half-mile marker, where the horses were to start their workout. Cindy gripped Honor's mane, preparing for the filly's sudden burst of speed.

Before Cindy could adjust her position over Honor's neck, Beautiful Music roared by them on the outside. Honor instantly charged in pursuit, switching to her right lead as she followed the black filly, moving to the outside of the track.

Cindy swayed dangerously in the saddle as Honor's lunge threw her to the left. She clenched her hands in Honor's mane, trying desperately to stay in the saddle.

The filly's strides were steady as she pounded after Beautiful Music. With a swift lurch Cindy righted herself in the saddle. Her arm responded with a flaming burst of pain, but Cindy knew she and Honor were okay now. Honor was gaining on Music with every stride. "Good," Cindy called. "Take her, girl!"

Barely a furlong from the finish, Honor suddenly seemed to decide to put Beautiful Music away. The bay filly's change in speed was so sudden and dramatic, Cindy almost fell backward out of the saddle. "That's it, girl!" she cried.

Honor showed no sign of stopping. In a second she was across the finish, three lengths ahead of Beautiful Music.

"Wow!" Mark called from behind them.

Cindy pulled up Honor and turned to him. "What happened back there, Mark? When you took off early, I just about got dumped!"

"I'm sorry," Mark apologized. "Music took off on

me—I almost fell off, too. But what a finish! I mean, Music's got talent, but Honor's in a class by herself."

Cindy trotted Honor over to the gap, eager to find out their time for the workout. Cindy knew that her dad and the official track clocker had timed Honor's run.

Honor pranced smartly along the track, bowing her well-muscled neck. Cindy smiled at the young horse's confidence.

"A tick over forty-seven seconds," Ashleigh called. Ashleigh was leaning on the fence next to Ian and Mike.

"That's fantastic, girl!" Cindy patted the filly's rump.

"Especially since you almost fell off," Ian said wryly.

"I'll just make sure I stay with her on race day," Cindy grinned. She slid to the ground and hugged Honor tight. The filly fondly rubbed her black muzzle against Cindy's side.

"Well, don't forget that a race is different from an exercise session," Ian cautioned. "You're going to be out there with seven other fillies, not one. And they're going to be jockeying for position and out for the win."

"It's hard to say with fillies this young, but some of them probably have as much talent as Honor," Ashleigh added. "Don't underestimate them, Cindy."

"I won't," Cindy said, trying not to feel too cocky about her chances.

Cindy saw the track doctor beckoning from the finish line. Her stomach tightened as she headed over to him. If he'd seen any sign of injury, he'd ground her for sure.

The doctor was writing on a notepad as Cindy approached, leading Honor. At last he looked up. "Okay," he said. "You can ride. I know you jockeys like to get right back out there. But be careful."

"I will. Thank you!" Beaming, Cindy turned Honor and walked her briskly toward the backside.

"Not a bad ride," a familiar voice said from behind her.

Cindy spun around, shocked. Jeremy was leaning casually against the rail. "Thanks," she said uneasily, trying to cover her surprise.

"How've you been, Cindy?" he asked. "I was a little surprised the track doctor cleared you to ride."

"I'm totally recovered," she lied. Her arm really hurt.

"Should be a good race next Saturday," Jeremy said.

"Which one?" Cindy asked coolly. "There's a full card of racing on Saturday."

Jeremy laughed. "*Our* race," he said. "The Magnolia. I'm riding in a couple of other races that day, but that's the one I'm looking forward to. I'm riding a dynamite filly—Magic Wand. Maybe you've heard of her."

"Of course I've heard of her." Cindy's throat suddenly felt dry. "I didn't know *you* were riding her," Cindy added. "I thought Denny Sonntag was."

Jeremy winked. "Last-minute change of rider. Her owner thought she deserved the best."

"Oh." Cindy gulped. Jeremy's words reminded her that she was still an apprentice jockey, and one who had suffered a debilitating injury. Unconsciously Cindy moved her right hand to massage her left shoulder.

Jeremy pushed himself off the fence. "Well, see you around," he said.

Cindy nodded casually. "Yeah, in the race—if not before. Come on, Honor." The filly agreeably moved off behind her.

Ashleigh fell into step beside them. "What did Jeremy have to say?" she asked.

"I just found out he's riding in the Magnolia," Cindy replied.

"So did I," Ashleigh said.

Cindy frowned. Whatever she thought of how Jeremy had handled Honor, she knew that he was considered a good rider. "Do you think that's a problem?" she asked. "He's riding Magic Wand."

Ashleigh shook her head. "Don't let him psych you out. Your chances are great on a horse like Honor— and her chances are great with a jockey like you aboard. Don't forget that."

"I won't." Cindy looked back at Honor, her determination rising. *Jeremy's not going to stop us after we've come this far!* she thought. *Nothing is.*

*   *   *

"I've been hearing good reports about you," Dr. Kandel said to Cindy the next afternoon. Cindy and Max sat in his office, and Cindy had finished her exercises. She had just glowingly described yesterday's black-type workout with Honor—the filly had been the fastest of the day, and so her name and time appeared in black type in the racing publications. "I'm so glad things are going well and that you're happy," the therapist added.

"I am happy," Cindy assured him.

"She is," Max agreed. "Sleepy sometimes, but happy." Cindy pretended to punch him.

"I don't want to burst your bubble, but I have to interject a note of caution," Dr. Kandel said. "As I've said before, the pain that you're feeling is a sign your arm isn't fully healed yet."

"How did you know I'm in pain?" Cindy asked. She'd thought she'd hidden it pretty well. But her arm hadn't stopped hurting since Honor's workout yesterday.

The therapist shrugged. "You hesitated when you were doing your exercises. It's good to push yourself—you'll make progress that way. But don't overdo it."

"I kind of have to when I'm riding Honor," Cindy admitted. "She's a lot of horse."

"Don't keep going if the pain is too much," Dr. Kandel warned. "Remember that your shoulder could break again."

Cindy shivered. She'd gotten so used to riding with pain, she'd forgotten how much danger that pain could mean. "Okay," she said. "I can't let that happen."

"Good luck in your race." Dr. Kandel stood and smiled as Cindy and Max left his office.

Cindy took a deep breath once they reached the parking lot. "That wasn't good news," she said.

"It wasn't anything you don't know, was it?" Max asked, leaning against his car. He raised his eyebrows.

"Not really." Cindy sighed. "I just wish he'd stop trying to scare me—now I *am* scared!"

Max squeezed her hand. "There's no point in thinking about it too much. Why don't we get some ice cream? There's an excellent place not far from here."

"Good idea." Cindy managed a smile.

But even ice cream couldn't get Cindy's mind off Dr. Kandel's warning. Cindy spooned the cherry off the top of her sundae and set it in Max's dish. "Maybe everyone has a point with all their warnings. Maybe I *shouldn't* ride Honor in the Magnolia," she said thoughtfully. "I really may not be up to it."

"Cindy, you're well enough to ride in the race or your doctor and the track doctor wouldn't have okayed you to ride," Max pointed out.

"But Max, I've—I've lied to everybody when I said my arm doesn't hurt anymore," Cindy whispered.

"I've never been afraid before a race before, but this time I really am."

"You've gotten this far," Max argued. "You can do it, Cindy."

"You know, it's funny." Cindy toyed with her spoon. "Before the accident with Honor, I was always afraid that the horses I rode would get hurt, not me. I guess that's because I always thought they might be put down, while I'd always heal." She smiled wryly. "Not true, huh?"

Max reached across the table and took her hands in his. "You're well enough to ride in that race. Don't you know that?"

"I know it's something I have to do," Cindy said with determination. "Now I just have to get out there and do it."

14

On the afternoon of the Magnolia race, Cindy ran a brush through Honor's tail, sweeping out a few stray pieces of straw, and stepped back. In a few minutes Ian and Ashleigh would come to the stall to escort Cindy and Honor to the saddling paddock, and shortly after that Honor would race.

Cindy dropped the brush and retrieved it with a trembling hand. "We're ready, aren't we, girl?" she asked. After thoroughly grooming Honor, Cindy had changed into the blue-and-white jockey silks of Whitebrook and come back for the filly.

Her dad and Ashleigh walked up behind her. "How's Honor doing?" Ian asked.

Cindy shook her head. "She's hyped up."

"It's really not surprising," Ian said reassuringly. "She's probably figured out it's race time, and she's still very inexperienced."

"I guess." A good part of the filly's behavior could definitely be attributed to inexperience, but Cindy knew that the filly was as nervous as she was.

"Come on, sweetheart," she said as calmly as she could. "Time to go to the saddling paddock."

Honor paced obediently behind Cindy toward the saddling paddock. A race had just ended, and the horses were returning with their trainers and grooms from the track. They were breathing hard, and sweat darkened their necks and flanks.

Honor twisted her head to look. "Yes, those horses just raced," Cindy said. "They look hot, but they had a good run, just like you will."

She glanced at Honor. The filly was almost as sweaty as the horses they had just passed, and she hadn't set a hoof on the track yet. *Just the way she was before the Debutante,* Cindy thought nervously.

Mike was waiting at the saddling paddock. "We'll get her ready, Cindy," Ashleigh said. "Go wait in the walking ring."

Cindy nodded. "I think Honor and I are just making each other jumpy."

"Neither of you have any reason to be nervous," Ashleigh said firmly. "Just give the race your best shot, the way you always do."

The way I always did, Cindy corrected her silently.

A few minutes later she watched as her dad and Mike led Honor out of the saddling paddock into the walking ring and circled her before the crowd. To her dismay, Cindy saw that the filly was so hot now, she was lathered. The day was overcast and humid, but none of the other fillies in the ring were sweating. Cindy twisted her hands with worry.

Magic Wand marched by after her trainer, an older man named Andrew Fahey, who was one of the leading trainers in Kentucky. The big brown filly seemed cool and confident. "Just like Jeremy," Cindy murmured.

"Did I hear my name?" Jeremy asked from behind her.

Cindy flushed and whirled around. "Um . . . no," she said innocently.

Jeremy winked. "My mistake. Well, I'm glad I ran into you, Cindy. Best of luck in the race."

"Good luck to you, too," she said politely, hoping he would go away.

Jeremy laughed. "Oh, I won't need luck," he said.

"What's going on?" Max had stepped up protectively behind Cindy.

Cindy shook her head, glad Max was there. "Nothing," she said. "We were just talking about the race."

Andrew Fahey led over Magic Wand. "Here's the winner," Jeremy said. "See you after the finish, Cindy."

Jeremy mounted up and rode off just as Honor was walking over. Cindy quickly compared the two fillies. Magic Wand was taller than Honor, but not a bit better muscled. Honor's golden coat gleamed in the gray day, and her perfect head, with its broad forehead and tapering muzzle, turned from side to side as she scanned the paddock area.

"She's looking for you," Max said.

"I'm looking for her, too." Cindy stepped forward, filled with love for her filly and determination to win the race.

Honor stopped just in front of Cindy and dropped her head so that they were eye to eye. "Hi, girl," Cindy said, meeting the filly's soft gaze. "Ready to go?"

Honor nuzzled her gently. The buzz of the excited crowd, the quick snorts of the eager, high-strung young horses, and the concerned expressions of her family and friends faded into the background. She and Honor were alone together, loving and trusting each other absolutely. Cindy knew it was a bond that could never be broken.

"It's time to mount up, Cindy," Ashleigh said quietly. Glancing up, Cindy saw from Ashleigh's face that the older jockey understood her feelings.

Mike gave her a leg into the saddle. Cindy quickly adjusted her stirrups and gathered the reins. "Okay," she said. "I'm set."

Ian looked up at Cindy with a frown. "Are you sure you're going to be all right?"

Cindy nodded, but she was watching Honor closely. The filly had begun to act jittery again, swinging her hindquarters and prancing on her front feet.

"The rail's playing out fast today," Mike said. "I'd take Honor there as soon as you can, Cindy."

"Right." Cindy had seen that herself in the races she'd watched earlier that day. But she shuddered at the thought of trying to point Honor at the rail.

"I know you will." Ashleigh reached up to pat Cindy's knee. "See you in the winner's circle."

Cindy smiled gratefully. "Let's go, Honor," she said.

The filly lunged in the direction of the track. With difficulty Cindy brought her down from a hopping canter to a walk, but Honor still dragged on the reins. Cindy winced as she had to apply more pressure to Honor's mouth. Cindy's arm didn't hurt yet—but she knew it would. "I wish I thought this meant you're raring to run, Honor," she murmured. "But I think you're just too nervous to stand still."

The filly sprang onto the track, and Cindy guided her by the stands for the post parade. As they passed the spectators filling the stands Honor began cantering almost in place again and snatching at the bit, trying to run.

"You definitely know this is a real race," Cindy said, trying to soothe the filly with her familiar voice. "But it won't be like last time with Jeremy, girl, I promise. Just settle down."

The filly flung up her head, tossing her black forelock. *Don't panic*, Cindy thought, unsure whether she meant herself or Honor.

Cindy rode away from the stands and toward the gate positioned on the backstretch. She was relieved to be away from the onlookers' close inspection. She knew her dad must be worried sick by now.

The attendants quickly loaded the horses into the gate, starting with the horse in the first slot. Cindy circled Honor, moving the filly clockwise to rest her left hand, as they waited for their turn to load.

Honor hesitated at the gate, then rushed into the stall, almost hitting the metal front. The back of the gate clanged shut behind them. "Here we go," Cindy said quietly, positioning herself over the filly's neck and gripping Honor's soft mane. Cindy knew that the gate would flip open the second the last horse loaded. She had to be ready for Honor's huge first stride in the race.

Cindy glanced to her left. Jeremy and his filly had drawn a post far to the outside. Abruptly Honor pawed the ground, hitting her knee on the front of the gate. The filly jumped back—and smacked her rump against the back door.

"Easy, easy!" Cindy soothed. Honor's ears flicked back in response, then pricked again. Cindy could tell Honor was trying to listen through her fear. But the filly still wasn't balanced on all four legs.

"Honor isn't set!" Cindy cried to the gate attendants, but the next second the gate crashed open anyway. Honor hurled herself midair, hitting her head on the side of the gate.

"Oh, my God!" Cindy cried. Off balance, Honor landed with a jarring thud, almost slinging Cindy off to the right. Wrenching her body upright, Cindy barely had time to bring Honor around hard to the left, narrowly avoiding a collison with a gray filly named Long Island Lady.

Cindy concentrated on Honor, trying to evaluate if she'd been hurt in her break from the gate. But Honor gathered her legs beneath her and charged after the field. "She's okay!" Cindy whispered thankfully. In a matter of moments Honor had closed the gap to the tightly bunched pack thundering across the backstretch.

In an instant they were in the midst of the race. Cindy quickly sized up the roaring confusion ahead of them. Skip the Dance, a black, was running on the lead by about four lengths. Pressing right behind her were Sapphire Isle and Winter's Queen, a dark chestnut and another black filly. Jeremy and Magic Wand were about two lengths ahead of Honor and were running wide in fourth. The other three fillies in the field formed a wall directly in front of Honor.

Honor swept up on the three trailing fillies. "Good, Honor," Cindy choked out. The heavy cloud of dust from the other fillies' hooves was suffocating. "We'll have to go around them—we've got to get to the rail!"

As if she understood, Honor abruptly cut across the track to the inside. Gripping the reins tight, Cindy moved her more gradually toward the rail. In just a few strides they'd passed the three trailers and were coming up on the turn—and the heels of Sapphire Isle and Winter's Queen. Magic Wand was still running wide and behind them.

Sapphire Isle and Winter's Queen were bearing out on the turn. Cindy saw a hole on the rail plenty big enough for Honor to slip through. "Now's our chance, Honor!" Cindy cried.

"And it's still Skip the Dance by one, with Sapphire Isle and Winter's Queen up close second, battling it out," the announcer called. "But there goes Magic Wand!"

Cindy looked quickly to her right and gasped. Magic Wand's hooves were right in Honor's face—Jeremy was going for the opening on the rail, too! Without hesitating, Cindy pulled Honor hard toward the inside and flattened herself against the filly's neck, asking her for all the speed she had.

But Magic Wand plunged through the hole first. Honor valiantly followed as fast as she could, almost running up on the heels of the other filly. Cindy was forced to check her. *Try to understand what I'm asking you to do, Honor,* Cindy begged silently. *I had a reason for asking you to run as fast as you can and then slow down!*

The next second Cindy realized that the filly had understood perfectly. She was powering through the hole right behind Magic Wand and passed Sapphire Isle and Winter's Queen!

"Now we're getting somewhere," Cindy muttered.

Her arm really hurt from pulling the strong filly to the inside to make the pass, but she ignored the pain. She concentrated on the horses in front of them.

"Skip the Dance has a lead of one, but in a bold move Magic Wand moves into second and is gaining on the inside," the announcer said. "Honor Bright is holding in third."

Snorting loudly, Honor stayed right behind Magic Wand on the rail. Skip the Dance was slowing as she rounded the turn—the fast early pace had burned her out, Cindy guessed. Now Magic Wand was on the lead! In the next moment Honor swept by tiring Skip the Dance on the inside.

"Only Magic Wand to go," Cindy whispered. "We won't let her kick dirt in our face, will we, Honor?"

In answer Honor closed the distance to within inches of Magic Wand. As the brown filly rounded the turn heading into the stretch, she took it a little wide. A tiny hole opened up on the rail!

Cindy knew that in seconds the hole would be gone. Magic Wand would enter the stretch, and Jeremy would straighten her out on the rail. Honor's last chance of winning would be gone—Cindy doubted if her filly had enough left to take Magic Wand on the outside after the difficult trip they'd already had.

But the gap between the rail and Magic Wand is so small! Cindy thought frantically. She and Honor ran a major chance of hitting either the rail or Magic Wand if the other filly moved over even a little. Honor hesitated, too.

In a split second Cindy made her decision. "Do it, Honor!" she cried, pulling the filly to the inside. The pain in her left arm almost made her black out, but she forced herself to stay conscious.

The filly responded, diving through the hole in an explosion of speed. She was on the lead! Cindy's arm was almost limp with strain, but by sheer will she kept it poised over Honor's neck.

"Honor Bright has made a huge move," the announcer called. "She's stormed past Magic Wand! But Magic Wand is answering, folks. Here she comes!"

Cindy didn't have to look to know what had happened. Magic Wand had found another gear and was flying up on Honor's outside. The other filly took the lead by a length, and she was drawing away! "No," Cindy cried. "Honor, you've got to have more!"

The young horse was almost exhausted. Her black mane slapped against her wet, gleaming neck, and her strides were labored. But her ears swept back, listening to Cindy's words. The next second Cindy felt Honor gather herself, as if she were reaching way down inside for strength. Digging in deep, she roared after Magic Wand with less than a furlong to go to the wire!

Honor was eating into Magic Wand's lead.... Honor had taken the lead by a nose! Cindy fought desperately to keep from swaying in the saddle.

"And it's Honor Bright on the lead, in a dazzling rush!" the announcer said.

Cindy gripped her left rein tighter, struggling to keep Honor from drifting out and into the other filly. Fresh pain shot through her arm. *I can't take any more!* she thought wildly.

Honor rushed toward the finish, but Cindy could feel the filly start to labor again. The pain in Cindy's arm was so excruciating, she could hardly think of anything else. Through a blur of tears she saw the finish line. "Just a few more strides . . . ," Cindy whispered, almost blinded by her tears. "Hold on, Honor. I will if you will!"

Magic Wand was even with Honor's shoulder, then her neck.

The wire flashed by. "After a long duel between Honor Bright and Magic Wand, the Whitebrook filly wins it!" the announcer called.

"We did it," Cindy could barely whisper. Tears were running freely down her cheeks as she clung to Honor's neck, trying to stay aboard. She didn't have the strength to pull the filly up.

Seeming to understand, Honor slowed herself and did a wide, smooth turn, bringing Cindy back to the gap at an easy gallop. "You did that for me, didn't you?" Cindy whispered, overcome with love for her filly. "You're my Honor. Thanks so much, girl!" Cindy smiled through her tears.

The Whitebrook group, grinning and cheering,

had gathered at the gap. Cindy saw their expressions change to ones of concern as she got closer. Max and Ashleigh ran out onto the track. Ashleigh took Honor's reins as Cindy crumpled in the saddle, then slid down into Max's waiting arms. She knew she would have fallen if he hadn't been there. "All right, Cindy!" he said softly.

"Are you okay?" Ashleigh asked anxiously.

"My arm," Cindy whispered hoarsely. "It hurts so much. Max, do you think I broke it again?"

With gentle fingers Max massaged her shoulder. "No, I don't. If it was broken, you wouldn't have made it back here—you'd be lying out there on the track."

"I came close to that." Cindy turned quickly to Honor. Her dad stood next to Cindy now, beaming. "Is Honor okay? She gave everything she had out there."

Honor was huffing out soft, quick breaths, but she seemed calm and happy, totally unlike the jumpy filly who had first stepped onto the track this afternoon. She rubbed her black velvet muzzle against Cindy's cheek.

"She's fine," Ian said. He kissed Cindy's forehead. "I'm so proud of you, honey."

Beth, holding Kevin, and Samantha were struggling through the crowd. "Cindy, you were wonderful!" Beth called. Reaching Cindy's side, she held out a cold can of soda. "Relax and enjoy, sweetheart."

"Good job, sis," Samantha added.

"Thanks." Cindy tipped back her head, letting the cold liquid soothe her dry throat. She did feel better.

Ashleigh was talking to the press. Cindy took Honor's reins from Max. "Let's go hear what they're saying," she said to Honor.

Honor tossed her head vigorously and snorted, looking every inch the proud, confident racehorse. She marched after Cindy to a chorus of oohs and ahs from the crowd.

"We'll definitely point Honor at more races this summer," Ashleigh was saying to a reporter. "The Spinaway at Saratoga at the end of August is a possibility. Of course, Cindy McLean will definitely be her jockey."

"Wow!" Cindy grinned broadly at the mention of the grade-one race at the famous old Saratoga track. Max gave her a thumbs-up.

Honor twisted her pretty head to look at Cindy. The filly's eyes were bright, as if she wanted to know, "What do you think?"

Cindy hugged Honor's golden neck tight. "You're on your way, girl," she said. "I know you're going to be Whitebrook's next champion!"

Don't miss the exciting adventures of a new generation of Thoroughbred horses and riders at Whitebrook Farm!

Ashleigh's daughter, Christina Reese, and her friends are crazy about horses. Whether they're jumping a cross-country course, riding an exacting dressage test, or galloping a powerful racehorse to a thrilling victory, only one thing matters: the special bond between horse and rider.

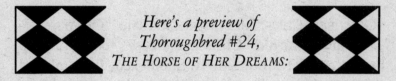

Here's a preview of Thoroughbred #24, The Horse of Her Dreams:

Christina has spent her whole life around horses. But she's not planning to follow in her mother's footsteps and become a jockey. Christina wants to be an event rider. The only thing that stands in her way is having the perfect horse. She takes her first step toward competing in an event when she gets to ride her trainer's horse, Foster. But back home, her own pony teaches her an important lesson about aiming too high, too fast. . . .

"GO AHEAD, CHRIS," HER INSTRUCTOR SAID. "CANTER ON."

Twelve-year-old Christina Reese took a deep breath and let it out slowly. She flexed, then relaxed the muscles in her arms and back so the horse wouldn't pick up on her anxiety. Then she shortened her reins and gave Foster a bump with her outside leg, dreading what might happen next.

To her amazement, the horse cantered flawlessly right out of the walk. A grin spread across Christina's face as she realized Foster's canter was as smooth as syrup. On her pony, Tribbles, Christina felt every footfall of his short strides. But the steady three-beat rhythm of Foster's canter was muted in rhythm and power.

She swept around the turn where Dylan stood, and this time she saw unmistakable admiration in his

164

face. When her back was to him, her grin broke into a big smile, and she knew she could ride this horse, bouncy trot and all; she was going to be just fine.

The rest of the day Christina thought about riding Mona's horse. She was telling her best friend, twelve-year-old Kevin McLean, all about it as they rode along the fence line in one of the pastures at Whitebrook.

"And then she let me try jumping him!" Christina said enthusiastically.

"How high?" Kevin wanted to know.

"Not very high," Christina admitted. "Just a cross rail and then a little vertical. But I'm going to jump higher," she assured him. "Mona said so."

"That's great," Kevin said.

They rode along in silence for a while, enjoying the sunshine and the clean smell of the fresh grass. "So . . . do you know Dylan Becker?" Christina asked Kevin.

"Sure," Kevin said. "He's on the basketball team. And I play baseball with him in the summer. He's pretty good," Kevin added, looking at her curiously. "Why?"

"No reason," Christina said, suddenly embarrassed. She wished she hadn't said anything. Before them, twenty yards away, was a wooded section of the pasture. "Hey, you want to do the steeplechase course?" Christina said, glad for a chance to change the subject.

"Okay," Kevin agreed quickly. "The loser has to buy sodas."

"Deal," Christina said.

"But I warn you," Kevin said mischievously, "I have a need for speed."

"No fear," Christina said coolly as she gathered up Trib's reins. The pony's ears pricked forward as he anticipated what was about to happen. "Ready?" Christina asked Kevin.

"Just say when," Kevin said, poised to gallop.

"Go!" Christina yelled.

Christina and Trib took off across the grass toward the trees, with Kevin and his horse right beside them. The "steeplechase course" was really a trail through the trees that Christina and Kevin had placed obstacles across. They had been racing each other over the course since they were old enough to ride by themselves.

Christina snuck a glance at Kevin and Jasper as they approached the woods. Jasper was fast, but she knew that Trib could beat him. That is, if she and Trib could get to the woods first.

The two horses galloped neck in neck as they approached the path. But once they were actually in the woods, they would have to go single file. Christina knew from experience that whoever was in front when they hit the trail would be the winner, and she bent forward, urging Trib to go faster. At the entrance to the path, Jasper pulled ahead and Christina had to check Trib to keep from bumping Jasper's hindquarters as he dodged ahead of them into the trees.

"Shoot!" Christina grumbled.

"Gotcha!" she heard Kevin holler as Jasper thundered down the trail in front of her.

"Not for long!" she yelled as Trib pounded after them.

The first obstacle was the low, smooth trunk of a tree that had fallen across the trail. Jasper sailed over it, and Trib sprang over it right behind him. Several strides farther on was a small pile of brush and branches. Both horse and pony bounded over it. The third jump was just a tree branch set across the path, it ends resting in the low branches of the bushes on either side. It was little more than a stick about two and a half feet high, with nothing but air under it, but Jasper and Trib knew it was there and cleared it without missing a beat.

In the straight stretch after the branch jump Christina and Trib began to gain on Kevin and Jasper. Trib nearly had his face in the sorrel gelding's flaxen tail as they pounded toward a turn. Christina moved up on the inside as they headed into the bend in the path, preparing to sneak by where the path widened for a brief stretch. Clucking to Trib, she moved her hands forward, asking him for a burst of speed.

The pony doubled his strides, surging past Jasper, then ducking in front of the horse just as the path straightened out and narrowed again.

"Hey!" Kevin said indignantly.

Howling with laughter, Christina thundered toward the next jump, two Christmas trees with their tops pointing at each other across the trail. She could hear

Jasper's hoofbeats right behind them as they came to the last jump, but she knew she had them beat.

Three strides after they cleared the branch pile, Christina broke through the trees into the sunlight again. In front of her was the "homestretch"—a long lane of grass leading to the top of a hill. If she could keep the lead until they reached the hilltop, they would win.

She dug her legs into Trib's sides and thundered up the stretch, sure she had Kevin beat. But when she glanced over her shoulder, she saw that Jasper was right beside her and moving up, his longer legs slowly but surely outstriding Trib. Kevin was laughing as they pulled past.

"Get up!" she ordered Trib, and gave him a smack on the shoulder with her bat. The pony shook his head in annoyance but then seemed to dig in and find more speed. Trib's mane stung Christina's face as she leaned into his gallop, trying to get over the crest of the hill before Kevin.

She was squinting into the sun and wind when she saw the dark shape looming in front of her. For a moment she was confused, then she remembered the fallen tree she had seen from the training oval that morning. The trunk of the tree lay directly in their path. Kevin was on her left; he could move over and go the shorter distance around the broken stump. Christina realized she would either have to drop back and follow him or go all the way around the top of the tree to her right. Either way, she would lose.

Kevin glanced over at her, and she could see from his expression that he was thinking the same thing.

Christina hated to lose. "Okay, Trib," she muttered. "There's only one way to win this."

She shortened her reins a little and aimed her pony right for the center of the fallen tree. Several leafy branches stuck up from the trunk, but there was one narrow section that was clear.

They reached the tree. Kevin swerved left, around the stump, and Christina fixed her eyes on the trunk. Trib cantered all the way to the base of it without missing a beat. She rested her hands on the crest of his neck, prepared to feel him spring into the air and over the tree. Christina grinned, thinking how surprised Kevin would be when he came around the stump and saw that she had jumped the tree and pulled ahead of him.

But she was completely unprepared for what happened next. . . .

KAREN BENTLEY rode in English equitation and jumping classes as a child and in Western equitation and barrel-racing classes as a teenager. She has bred and raised Quarter Horses and, during a sojourn on the East Coast , owned a half-Thoroughbred jumper. She now owns a red roan registered Quarter Horse with some reining moves and lives in New Mexico. She has published fourteen novels for young adults.